KONSTANTIN

TOM BULLOUGH

PENGUIN BOOKS

PENGUIN BOOKS

Published by the Penguin Group
Penguin Books Ltd, 80 Strand, London WC2R ORL, England
Penguin Group (USA) Inc., 375 Hudson Street, New York, New York 10014, USA
Penguin Group (Canada), 90 Eglinton Avenue East, Suite 700, Toronto, Ontario,
Canada M4P 2Y3 (a division of Pearson Penguin Canada Inc.)
Penguin Ireland, 25 St Stephen's Green, Dublin 2, Ireland (a division of Penguin Books Ltd)
Penguin Group (Australia), 707 Collins Street, Melbourne, Victoria 3008, Australia
(a division of Pearson Australia Group Pty Ltd)
Penguin Books India Pvt Ltd, 11 Community Centre, Panchsheel Park, New Delhi – 110 017, India
Penguin Group (NZ), 67 Apollo Drive, Rosedale, Auckland 0632, New Zealand
(a division of Pearson New Zealand Ltd)
Penguin Books (South Africa) (Pty) Ltd, Block D, Rosebank Office Park, 181 Jan Smuts Avenue,
Parktown North, Gauteng 2193, South Africa

Penguin Books Ltd, Registered Offices: 80 Strand, London WC2R ORL, England

www.penguin.com

First published by Viking 2012
Published in Penguin Books 2013
001

Copyright © Tom Bullough, 2012
All rights reserved

The moral right of the author has been asserted

Typeset by Jouve (UK), Milton Keynes
Printed in England by Clays Ltd, St Ives plc

ISBN: 978–0–670–92093–8

KONSTANTIN

Tom Bullough was born in 1975 and is the author of two previous novels. He lives in Breconshire, in mid-Wales, with his wife and young son.

For Edwyn

The greater man's progress, the more he replaces
the natural by what is artificial

Konstantin Tsiolkovsky,
Dreams of Earth and Sky (1895)

Little Bird

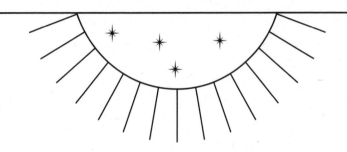

December 1867

Kostya hurried down the bank towards the frozen Oka, fine and light in his heavy sheepskin coat as a sparrow in its winter plumage. On the river, the tracks of the woodsmen cut north through the even snow, steering a line towards the pine logs strewn along the shore beneath the forest. Kostya ran and slid on the exposed ice. From the darkness of the birch trees he emerged in the December sunlight, one arm extended for balance, the soup can blazing between his shirt and his coat, and nowhere beneath the ice-blue sky could he see any movement beside his own long, wavering shadow.

The snow on the north bank had formed a crust since it was last trampled by horses and men in bast shoes, and the boy moved quickly and easily up the slope. He climbed among white-capped logs in their hundreds, which would, in the spring, be carried east with the broken ice, seething and roaring the 350 versts to the sawmills at Nizhny Novgorod, but for now were as frozen as the forest behind them. Their tracks in the deep snow were broad, hard and sparkling, cutting between the bare, scrubby lilacs and the gangling ash trees – converging on a door in the wall of the pines.

That winter, as everyone in Ryazan knew, felling had been prohibited within five versts of the river. Even for a grown-up it was an hour's walk to the woodcutters' clearing, and Kostya arrived in the forest almost at a trot, following the plumes of his breath. In the gloom of the great, snow-laden trees, the cold was sharper than ever against his pink, rounded cheeks, his determined, down-turning mouth, the black Tatar eyes that had come to him from his mother. He held the soup can firmly to his skinny stomach, and he looked up only once, when the Sun cut a line through the tangled branches and turned their snow into a torrent of light.

It was perhaps a verst, perhaps two, before Kostya came to a bright red streak in the track in front of him. He stopped, touched it with his old felt boot and found that it was sticky. The streak was startling against the uniform whiteness. It stretched and wove away from him, complicated by clods of fur, arching in the prints of the horses, and as Kostya lifted his head he found himself facing a tall, scruffy dog – its thick coat glinting with icicles, its colour such that it need only to have retreated a few paces to have vanished among the white-grey trunks.

On the narrow track beneath the shadow-hung trees, Kostya heard the tremor of his heart, the gasp of his breathing, the hush as a cascade of snow slipped from the treetops, but beneath these fragile noises he heard nothing: the great, indifferent silence of the forest. Distantly, he wondered why this dog had strayed so far from Korostovo, the village where it surely lived. Through the smell of cabbage soup, he smelt its hard, animal stink. He saw the half-eaten hare beneath its wide, webbed claws. He saw its pyramid ears, its muscular shoulders, the knife-like teeth between its thin black lips.

He saw the silence in its fire-coloured eyes.

*

The swathe cut by the men from Korostovo lay parallel with the Oka: a great, gaping space of broken trees and open sky where women in headscarves and children in well-patched rags were gathering branches beneath the few deformed or unwanted pines, the limes and rowans that stood exposed in the winter sunlight. The smoke rose straight from the woodsmen's fires, like the ghosts of the trees they had felled. In the mouth of the track, Kostya stood small and shivering, the peak of his blue woollen cap low above his eyes. To the south, the men were working steadily, the cold air loud with their axes. He watched them cut a notch above the root of each tree, and a higher notch on the opposite side. He watched them hammer in the wedge as the treetop started to waver, and as the branches met the ground in a screaming, splintering crash he saw them fall upon the trunk – working with brisk, practised movements, slicing the bark along its length, skinning it like an animal.

Several minutes passed and several women paused in their work to point and call to Kostya before the foreman came striding from the shallow shadow to the south. Eduard Ignatyevich was a broad, dark figure with a black-grey beard, a long black coat and a black felt cap that covered his cropped black hair. Even with a bracking hammer swinging from his big, gloved hand he looked as much like a priest as a forester.

'Konstantin?' He took his spectacles from his pocket and hooked the arms over his ears. 'What are you doing here?'

Kostya produced the soup can from his coat. He held it up to him with trembling hands, the steam coiling faintly from the lid.

'Konstantin,' his father repeated. His eyelids flickered, but his voice remained low, methodically Polish. 'Let me explain to you something very important, which I have explained to you in the past but you have clearly failed to understand. In the town, a man is a mind. That is to say, in the town he is an intellectual being. With a house, a fire and a reliable source of food, he is able to rise above his surroundings, to forget his physical self and devote himself to mental pursuits. Without the town, we would have no books, no telegraph, no railway. Because in the forest, a man is simply an animal with neither fur nor claws. Alone in the forest in the winter, he may consider himself to be in terrible danger. Do I make myself clear?'

Eduard Ignatyevich opened his tin cigarette case, lit a match and released a cloud of smoke, which shone in the light of the low Sun prowling through the southerly treetops. Kostya blinked to stop himself crying. He gave a little nod and his father put a hand to his back and propelled him towards a nearby bonfire where a pine tree stood like a visiting mourner – a rotten lip near the top of its trunk where it had once been struck by lightning.

'As you know,' he continued, 'the zemstvo has decided that there will be no more felling in Ryazan after the end of this week. As a result, I have a great deal of work to do. So, I would like you please to make a bed of embers and warm up your soup can, and then when it is hot I would like you to drink it.'

'But –' said Kostya.

'No buts.'

'But, Father, I brought it for you!'

'Konstantin,' said Eduard Ignatyevich, and his voice acquired the faintest edge. 'Do you take me for an idiot? Do you think that I come to the forest every day with inadequate food?'

'But . . . But, Mama said she was worried that you would have to work until after dark again. She said it's the most cold-est winter she can remember, and she said you would get hungry!'

His father turned at a shout from one of the woodsmen.

'Well,' he said, 'whatever your mother might have told you, I am quite sure that she had no intention that you should come all the way out here. Indeed, if she knows about it, I imagine she is losing her mind with worry. The situation is quite simple. You are shivering, which indicates that you are trying to remain warm. It is important that you do not catch a chill, therefore you are to drink the soup, stay by the fire and wait for me to return.'

Even with the heat from the bonfire, a skin of ice had already covered the small oval lenses of his spectacles.

*

It snowed again that night, and in the cold grey morning Voznesenskaya Street was clean and white beneath the low clouds, the shock-headed willows and the reds, blues and greens of the little houses. Once again the shutters were open. Women in shawls and aprons were clearing the paths to their doors, breathing visibly, remarking to one another on the twenty-five-degree frost, the ring that someone had seen around the Moon, the mouse that someone else had found in her shoe. Everyone, it seemed, had some portent of doom to report – although to Kostya, standing at the foot of the steps with his toboggan, the city looked very much the same as it had every other winter he could remember.

Kostya lived in a wooden house with vivid blue walls, three rectangular windows framed by a lacework of carving, and eaves that emerged from beneath the iron roof like the petticoats of some expensive lady. In the snow beside the door, there lay the remains of a thresher once invented by Eduard Ignatyevich, which had never successfully worked. From the squat brick chimney, a line of bluish smoke trailed west towards the embankment of the railway, which had come to Ryazan two and a half years earlier and would, said Kostya's mother, one day reach such places of the imagination as Voronezh and Rostov-on-Don: the very shores of the Black Sea!

'Ignat!' Kostya shouted.

The front door opened and his brother came skidding out

of the small dark kitchen where the ten members of the Tsiolkovsky family spent every night from October to April.

'You two mind that you don't catch cold!' their mother called
after him.

'Yes, Mama!'

Ignat was a couple of vershoks shorter than Kostya, a skinny
specimen, nine years old, with large blue eyes and a shadow in
his mouth where he had recently lost his front teeth. With barely
a year between them, the two boys had long been inseparable,
and they turned without a word along the tracks of a troika,
which happened to have passed that morning. They raised their
woollen hats to a neighbour who was loading hay through his
barn's stable door, a couple of chickens pecking imaginary
morsels at his feet, and as they passed the brightly painted houses
they summoned their friends with deafening whistles:

'Andrei!'

'Viktor!'

'Nikolai!'

'Come tobogganing!'

Myasnitskaya Street led north towards the centre of the city,
and it wasn't long before the two boys reached the limits of the
Fire of 1837, where the houses became tall, brick and stone,
muted shades of yellow and pink. One was the merchants' club,
where a group of men in bearskin coats were huddled in discus-
sion. Another was the hospital, where, faintly, Kostya could
make out the screams of some unfortunate patient. Beyond
the creaking sledge and steaming horse of an *izvozchik*, they
passed a team of peasants sweeping the wooden pavements in
the snow-smothered gardens of Novobazarnaya Square and
they steered as close as they could to a man selling meat pies –
the smell so sumptuous that it was almost worth the visit in
itself.

'Just imagine . . .' Kostya began.

'Kostya!'

'I know, I know. But I haven't got a kopeck.'

'You've got a twenty-kopeck coin! I know you have!'

'Well, you're not having that!'

'Then I'm not listening.'

'Oh, come on, Ignat!'

'You said you'd give me a kopeck every time I had to listen to one of your stories.'

For a moment they walked in silence.

'I'll tow you as far as Sobornaya Square,' said Kostya. 'How about that?'

Ignat sat down on the toboggan and pulled his knees up to his chest.

'Giddy up, horse!' he said.

'Right.' Kostya hauled on the string. 'Imagine if everything in Ryazan was the same size as us. If everything was really small, that would make us really big, wouldn't it? Then all the other people wouldn't even be able to see over our boots, but we could see right out over the rooftops. We'd be able to look straight into the fire-towers, and wouldn't the lookouts get a shock when they saw us!' He laughed delightedly. 'And they would have to be nice to us too, because we would be very, very strong and we could just pick up the whole tower if we wanted and plonk it in the river!'

'Faster!' Ignat tossed a snowball against his brother's back, and Kostya began to run – the big, stucco houses sliding steadily past them. From the north, the fifteen-minute whistle of the morning train cut through the freezing air.

'In my world, anyway, there wouldn't be any gravity, so it would be easy to pick up anything we liked. In my world, I would be able to jump versts through the air. I would be able to jump through the clouds and right out into the ether. If I wanted to go to Moscow, I would just have to run and jump and I could fly there, easy. The people in the train would see me zooming past like a cannonball! I would bring back a new dress for Mama, and a smart new fountain pen for Father, and a whole cow for us all to eat –'

'What would you bring me?' asked Ignat.

'I would bring you a toboggan as big as a kibitka, with red velvet seats and a bell on the front so that everyone would know you were coming!'

At Sobornaya Square, where an official in cloak and brass buttons was hurrying between the government offices, Kostya stopped beneath a lamp post. All morning he had felt as though something was caught in his throat, and as he coughed and tried to clear the obstacle he felt a sudden wash of giddiness and had to sit down on a bench – facing the avenue that converged on the golden campanile of the kremlin.

The best tobogganing slope in the whole of Ryazan was the bank of the Trubezh River, near Uspensky Cathedral, whose five deep blue, star-spotted cupolas were like the night sky seen from the outside. The river itself was derisory, a trickle compared to the great winding Oka, but to its south there rose a virtual cliff where, on any winter's day, you could find a mob of boys flying downhill on shovels and old doors, shrieking and spinning across the ice.

'Kostya!' called one. 'Is it true you went to the Korostovo fellings yesterday?'

'He did!' said Ignat.

'What, on his own?'

'Did you get a beating?'

'Their father never beats them, lucky buggers . . .'

'Oh! I would have caught it!'

'Poles!'

It was a matter of pride to Kostya that he possessed an actual toboggan. He had made it himself, and although it amounted to little more than two planks trimmed into curves and a third plank for a seat, he had nailed four wedges to the inside corners for strength, waxed the runners and decorated the sides with bits of coloured glass that he had found in the icon-makers' yard. As he strode through the crowd, he greeted his friends and took pleasure in their complimentary comments. Arriving at the slope, he considered the scars and footprints in the fresh snow. He sat down, dug his heels into the ground, waited for Ignat to squeeze between his legs, then walked them to the edge, leant forwards and lifted his feet.

Although both boys had come sledging here numberless times, still the first run of the day was enough to stop the breath in your throat. The ground dropped away so sharply that you might have been falling. Kostya clung to the string, his brother and the sides of the toboggan. He screwed up his eyes against the bitter wind and the flying snow, and as they hit the lip between the bank and the river he felt them lift clean into the air.

They landed, by chance, on both runners and sped away across the ice – past the quay where the steamboats docked in the summer, past the fishermen crouched over their holes with saw, line and bottle, past the shying horse of a cursing peasant and the final tracks of the other boys – and they hit the far bank with just enough speed to climb half an arshin up the slope.

Shaking with laughter, Kostya lay with his feet in the air and his head on the ice, his face burning, his cap, his linen trousers and his sheepskin coat all caked evenly in snow. Beyond the cross-topped domes of the kremlin and the skeletal beech trees that reached like roots into the clouds, a scrawl of black smoke stretched above the city. After a moment, the train's five-minute whistle sounded long and mournful, and just as other boys could tell a bird by its song so Kostya could tell that its engine was an o-6-o: a wood-burning freight locomotive with six drive wheels and no guiding axle – unstable at speed, but useful in these wintry conditions. The ice was forming on his collar, but still he gazed at the smoke in the sky, that signature of power. He thought of the roaring pistons and the steam that fled down the flanks of the carriages. He imagined himself travelling north, fast as a galloping horse – following the telegraph wires through Kolomna, Voskresensk and Lyubertsy, all the way to Moscow itself.

*

That afternoon, Kostya sat at the table in the kitchen and stared into the icon corner, where the logs of the walls met like fingers. As a rule, he enjoyed mathematics. He loved its music, the way that the answers would pop unbidden into his head. It was only today that the numbers seemed dark and evasive, shadowy through the ache in his throat and the pain in his head, and when his two younger sisters arrived from the yard with arms full of icicles he shivered so violently in the cold air from the open door that his chalk went skidding across the slate.

'"The stepmother knew very well . . ."' read Ignat, who was sitting beside him, running a finger across Afanasyev's *Tales*.

'Yes?' their mother prompted.

Ignat sucked air through the space in his teeth. '"The stepmother knew very well that . . . deep in the forest there was a . . . wr . . . a . . ."'

'Spell it out now.'

'W, R, E, T, C, H, E, D.'

'And what does that spell?'

'Wre . . . ? Wretched!'

'Very good!'

' "A wretched little hut with the legs of a hen. And . . . in that little hut, there lived a horrible old witch called Baba Yaga!" '

Even in the ice-softened daylight, Maria Ivanovna looked exhausted. There were lines between her arching eyebrows, around her tapering eyes, her high Tatar cheekbones. Her grey woollen dress was clean and pressed, but it hung unfilled beneath her milk-heavy breasts, and as she packed into an iron-bound trunk the work of philosophy that her husband wrote for an hour every evening, the strands of silver shone in her thick black hair.

'Mama?' said Kostya, eventually. 'Mama, I'm thirsty.'

His mother straightened up, one arm supporting her chest. 'Have you done your sums yet, Kostya?'

'Not . . . Not yet, Mama.'

'Then you can have a drink when you finish your sums.'

'But, Mama . . .'

Out by the frozen well, Masha and Fekla were singing a song that their mother had taught them on one of their countless long winter's evenings – the story of a prince and a beautiful changeling peasant girl. There was always more noise about the house when Eduard Ignatyevich was at work. Often Maria Ivanovna would sing herself, and when Kostya wasn't faced with such problems as $136 \div 8$ and 157×5 he would join in too, rattling between his various projects: the puppets and the model trains that he would make out of glue and cardboard, the cockroaches he would catch with Ignat and race along a floorboard framed by particularly wide cracks.

Today, however, the song was simply fuel to the pain in his head.

'Konstantin!' Maria Ivanovna was standing behind him, staring down at her own neat, rounded numbers and the line that had spat from his chalk. 'What on Earth have you done?'

'Mama,' he said, in a pitiful voice. 'I don't feel well.'

'You've crossed out my sums!'

'No, Mama! I didn't mean to!'

'By all that's holy, Konstantin!'

On the ledge above the stove, the baby started to cry.

Maria Ivanovna put her hands to her face, breathing heavily. 'Yesterday ... You've no idea ... Konstantin, I've told you endlessly not to go into the forest, haven't I? I've told you all about the dangers, and the risk of getting lost, and the robbers, and the Baba Yaga, and what do you do? You go off into the forest, on your own, right in the middle of winter!'

'But, Mama –'

'And now I ask you to do ten sums easily within your ability, and not only do you not even try to do them, for some reason you actually cross them out!'

'Mama, I don't feel well –'

'And what did I tell you when you left the house this morning? What did I specifically tell you?!'

'Not to catch cold, Mama,' said Kostya, miserably.

'Not to catch cold,' said his mother. 'And so, of course, you catch cold!'

Beside him, Ignat sat in silence, his finger on the page, his eyes turned furtively towards them. In the summer room, the girls came marching back among the barrels of pickled cabbage and cucumber, the model trains and houses that Eduard Ignatyevich had made himself when the older boys were small and he still had time for such diversions – their boots loud on the hollow floor, their voices shrill and penetrating.

'Honestly, Kostya, what on Earth am I supposed to do with

you? Do you not realize what a difficult time this is for us? Your father no longer has work here! Do you understand what that means? In five days he will be leaving for Vyatka. We are going to have to pack everything up and say goodbye to all of our friends, and travel all the way across the country, and . . .' She hesitated, her cracked red hands in fists against her belly. 'Well, your father may not approve of beating, but I was raised on it and, I swear, if you continue with this behaviour I will take your trousers down, bend you over and beat the life out of you!'

*

'I saw a wolf!' Kostya whispered.

Beside him, Ignat stirred in the broad straw bed. His eyelids quivered, his eyes fiery in the wind-raised light from the big stove.

'What . . . ?' he said, sleepily.

'I saw a wolf, in the forest!'

Kostya felt light, alert, as if he were dreaming. The pain in his head and his throat was gone. There was a distant discomfort in the bones of his limbs, but they seemed somehow to be the limbs of somebody else. He himself was perfectly composed. He was warm and safe in this strong little house with its fire and its food – apart from the blizzard that howled and clawed at the shutters, trying to force its way inside.

'Why didn't you tell me?'

'I was scared.'

'If you're telling me one of your stories . . .'

'I'm not! It's true!' Kostya's whisper broke into speech.

'Ssh!'

Behind Ignat's anxious, flame-painted face, Maria Ivanovna sighed with every breath – her head turned right, towards her guardian angel, and Anna, Fekla and Masha, and the fire-lit canopy that divided the kitchen every night. Faint through the thin linen, Eduard Ignatyevich lay between Alexei and Dmitri, muttering in Polish. Beneath the kerosene lamp, St Nikolai the Miracle Worker, St Ioann the Divine, the Weeping Virgin and Christ Pantocrator appeared to be suspended in the air – their faces lined equally with wisdom and suffering.

'What happened?' asked Ignat. 'How come it didn't eat you?'

But a weakness and a weariness had come over Kostya, quick as a cloud's shadow, and even as he opened his mouth to reply he felt himself sliding back into sleep.

*

Ivan Ivanovich Lesovsky was a kind old man, a Pole, a friend of Eduard Ignatyevich, but as he approached Kostya in the fluttering candlelight on that second evening he looked terrible, diabolic. Tall and stout, he had snow on his shoulders, shadow-filled craters beneath his eyes and a fine moustache that emerged from his beardless cheeks like little horns. He stood above the bed, his face carved from darkness, while Kostya shrank beneath the blanket until he could barely see over its edge.

'Hello, old chap.' He had a deep voice, almost subterranean. 'Can you tell me what's wrong? Have you got a sore throat?'

'Kostya, you know Dr Lesovsky.' Maria Ivanovna sat beside him, stroking the wet hair back from his forehead. She set a candle on a chair beside the bed and the shadows shrunk in the doctor's face. The light glittered on the ice in his moustache. Suddenly his expression was one of concern, so Kostya allowed his mother to pull the blanket back beneath his chin.

'Have you got a sore throat, Little Bird?'

Kostya nodded, and coughed up a thick, glue-like substance. The doctor smiled. He placed a hand on Kostya's forehead, then produced a gold watch from his waistcoat pocket and set two long hairy fingers on the inside of his wrist. He hummed a tune and watched the second hand make its circle of the face.

'One forty,' he pronounced. 'And I'd put the temperature at forty, forty and a half. You're not at all well, are you, poor old chap?' He turned to Maria Ivanovna. 'How long has he been like this?'

'He started complaining . . . yesterday, Ivan Ivanovich.'

'You didn't think to call me then?'

'Well . . .' She stroked Kostya's hair more urgently. 'You see, Ivan Ivanovich, he'd been playing in the snow. I thought he'd just caught a chill . . .'

The doctor took the candle and inspected Kostya's mouth and cheeks. The shadows moved through the pouches of his face and the tiny holes that pitted his large red nose.

'Well, old boy,' he said. 'I'm going to have to have a look down your throat, so we're going to have to get you out of bed. It won't hurt, don't worry. Do you think you can manage that?'

Thin and feeble in his long white shirt, Kostya pushed his legs over the edge of the mattress. He got to his feet with the help of his mother, while the doctor wrapped him in the blanket and lifted him on to her lap.

'Well done, Kostya,' she murmured. 'Well done, Little Bird . . .'

When Ivan Ivanovich put his fingers to the sides of Kostya's neck, the boy howled and thrashed against the blanket, but his arms were pinioned and his mother, even his mother, was holding his head so that he couldn't pull away. The doctor bent over him, the candle in one hand, and when he pushed a cold metal spoon between his lips it was as if his tongue were being sliced with razors. Mucus boiled in his throat, fetid and clinging. In the gale of his breath, the candlelight panicked. The doctor's face seemed to convulse, whipped up like the Oka in the fierce autumn winds, a flame in each eye and each dribbling icicle that hung from his moustache, and, realizing that he had been deceived, Kostya shook and fought and wailed in terror.

*

Later, when he was free to move again, Kostya lay limply across the big bed. His head lolled to the right, as his mother had left it. His eyes were closed, shivering faintly beneath their lids. He was tiny, translucent, a daub of violent colour on each cheek like a peasant girl at Easter.

'Maria Ivanovna,' said the doctor, patiently. 'You must understand that in your condition you cannot risk staying with him. You can't stay with him, he can't stay with the other children and none of you can stay in this house until it has been cleaned. The floors must be scrubbed, the walls whitewashed and your clothes and sheets washed and baked. I will send the watchman from the hospital with potassium permanganate, which should be dissolved in four buckets of water and left in the corners of the house for a week at least . . .'

'Would you like some more tea, Ivan?' asked Eduard Ignaty-evich in a low, tight voice.

Behind his eyelids, Kostya dozed, woke, dozed, skimmed the surface of sleep. His fingers twitched beneath the blanket. His breath croaked from his open mouth, while saliva trickled down his cheek and formed a dark circle on the white linen.

'*Pan doktor*, I've lost six children! Six! I cannot bear to lose another!'

Kostya did not feel his father dress him in trousers, boots, woollen hat and sheepskin jacket, and wrap him in the blanket. He woke only with the fearsome cold outside in the street, where great white flakes fell from the vastness of space, shining from a light cut to the shape of his mother, from the lantern that hung from a sledge whose driver had snow in piles on his hat and coat, whose horse stood shivering in the arch between the shafts. Eduard Ignatyevich's breath was hot and odourless. His beard was coarse against the tender skin of Kostya's face. His arms were knots of strength beneath his son's back and legs. As the whip flew out above the horse's back, Kostya heard himself groan and saw the snowflakes weaving from the blackness, like the stars falling from their homes.

> *Full well the Virgin trod the road*
> *That led her to Ryazan!*

Beside the tavern were figures with huge distorted faces, dancing in the snow with accordions and wheeling arms.

The church bells made a pulsing, shimmering roar.

'Nearly there, Kostya,' said his father, in a soft, unfamiliar voice. 'Nearly there now.'

The big stone houses formed a ravine, a cleft in the Earth where the snowflakes swarmed around the gas lamps. It was at its deepest point that Ivan Ivanovich's sledge passed between the lanterns on the gateposts of the hospital and stopped beside three steps, a pair of doors and a wall of light-leaking shutters. From inside, there came the familiar screams, and Kostya began to struggle feebly in his father's arms.

As they passed through the door, they met a torrent of noise and heat. Ivan Ivanovich shouted and gesticulated. The waiting room seethed and pressed towards him, peasants bowing and crossing themselves, long hair swinging across their raw, bearded faces. On the floor, one man lay in a puddle of blood, his legs impressed with the runners of a sledge, held together only by his trousers. On a bench a heavily pregnant woman was groaning, ignored. On another, a drunkard snored insensibly.

'I do appreciate your assistance, Eduard,' said Ivan Ivanovich, distantly. 'The feldshers are overwhelmed . . . We have a case of scarlatina, therefore the first thing to do is to reduce the swelling in the lymphatic glands. I will begin by decongesting the nostrils, and then relieve the throat by means of the principle of opposition.'

In a bare white room, Kostya lay naked on an oilcloth. Above him, a pressure lamp gave out such light and heat that his father and the doctor seemed unreal, angelic. His father's spectacles were lamps in themselves. Someone was sponging his body with warm water, moving across his legs and his abdomen, which were red and prickly like goose flesh. The doctor held some kind of pump – a glass cylinder with notches on the side – and when he set its mouth to Kostya's nose the boy felt an explosion of pain. Mucus and soapy water burst from the other nostril and spattered over his chin. He coughed and retched. He flapped like a fish on the slippery bed. In a moment, he saw his father's eyes, small and blue behind their lenses. Through the roar of the flame, he heard him speaking incomprehensibly, as if asking continual questions. He could smell again now – soap, kerosene and, to his surprise, potato – and when the doctor next appeared he was holding a bulging handkerchief. In the depths of his mind, Kostya remembered a trick that his sister Anna had once shown him, when she placed a ball inside a bottle, sealed the bottle, and then revealed it to be empty. In the flickering light, the doctor squeezed the handkerchief so that hot potato oozed between his fingers, and he pressed it to the agonized side of Kostya's neck, while ladling snow into his mouth.

January 1868

Kostya's room was tall but narrow. It contained a small black stove, a pile of logs, an icon of Vasily the Blessed, naked and supplicating, a bed with a golden dome at each corner and a chair where Ivan Ivanovich would appear periodically to frown, feed him water or push a wood-framed instrument into his armpit, which he would later return to consult. The room had a window with shutters that were sometimes closed and sometimes open. Once, Kostya managed to pull himself upright. With the heat from the stove the inside window was clear of ice, but even in the sunlight that made the 'T' out of 'KOSTYA' on the wall beside the door still the outside window remained opaque – the horses and patients who arrived in the yard the spectral inhabitants of a separate world.

There were worms in Kostya's head, which made him scream and attack the iron bed-end like he was fighting the bars of a cage. Some of them were curled like maggots in his throat, so that he struggled for every long, gargling breath and would wake from dreams in which he was being strangled. Others burrowed upwards into the bone and the matter of his brain until they came to his ears, where, pale, eyeless, sharp with spines, they gnawed at his flesh with little teeth. One night, when the shutters were closed and only the faint glow of the fire lit the room, Kostya pushed his fingers deep into his ears. He reached for the worms, and in the darkness felt a slick, slimy fluid dribbling from his earholes, down his neck, into the collar of his hospital shirt.

At one point that night, Kostya dozed and woke to find a faint slice of yellow light hanging in the air above him. He was calm, cool, for once without pain. His head lay on the pillow, but where formerly he had had shoulders and a ribcage now he had a tiny pair of arms thrown backwards and a pair of legs that curled above his belly to end in miniature feet. Kostya could feel every hair, every pore of his new skin in perfect detail. He knew that he was a baby, that he could neither stand nor speak. He lay helplessly, his fat hands open to the slice of yellow light, and so he remained for some unfathomable period of time, until the slice brightened into daylight and a memory of his previous body came back to him from a distant corner of the bed.

*

That afternoon, Kostya managed to drag himself to the chair beside the bed, and retrieved his twenty kopecks from the pocket of his sheepskin. The yellow-red sunlight cut into the room almost horizontally, colouring the smoke that leaked from the stove, leaving a yellow-red image of the window on the bare white wall beside the door. Kostya put the small cool coin on his swollen tongue and heard the silver click against his teeth. He swung open the inside window and inspected the yellow-red fronds of the ice on the outer pane. In the freezing air that poured across the bed, he wrapped his blanket round his shoulders, removed the coin from his mouth and, holding its edges with his fingernails, pressed it to the glass.

A perfect circle appeared in the light on the wall, containing a crown with a cross, a double-headed eagle with orb and sceptre, and a minute image of St George killing the dragon. When Kostya repeated the process with the other side of the coin, he made a second crown, a laurel wreath, the words '20 kopecks' and the date '1862'.

Kostya put his eyes to the two little circles and looked outside into the hospital yard. Between the gateposts and the silhouettes of the grand houses across the street, the Sun hung low and fierce above the shallow roofs of Ryazan. The snow was pink, like some expensive confection in the French shop on Novobazarnaya Square. The sunlight reduced the people in the runner-striped street to black, active shapes, like jackdaws. At the hospital steps, three men were loading a lifeless body on to a sledge – the horse spluttering, belching luminous clouds, stamping its feet on the hidden cobbles – and it was only when he heard the horse's noise that Kostya realized the hospital was silent. He frowned and listened again. Perhaps, he thought, it was New Year's Day. Perhaps all of the other patients had gone home to eat dumplings and porridge with jam.

Kostya pulled the blanket over his head like a shawl. After a time, there were footsteps on the hollow wooden floorboards in the corridor, but they did not stop at his door, and so to combat his loneliness he sang the song about the prince and the changeling girl. His voice was loud and muffled. With his blocked-up nose he had to stop to breathe at the end of every line. He scraped at the ice as it formed in his eyeholes, scanning the jackdaw figures for anyone he knew, and he became so involved in this world of shadows that he only noticed that the doctor had arrived when he felt him tap on his shoulder.

'Now then,' said Ivan Ivanovich, sternly. 'What do you think you're up to? You're ill, if you remember? It's minus ten degrees outside. That means, stay in your bed!'

He watched Kostya lie back on his pillow, then turned and sat down on the chair.

'Well?' he said.

'Yes, Ivan Ivanovich?'

'Are you going to stay in your bed?'

'Yes, Ivan Ivanovich,' said Kostya, meekly.

'Yes, Ivan Ivanovich.' The doctor paused then smiled, his clear pink lips revealing unruly teeth. 'So, how is the headache?'

'It's not as bad as it was, Ivan Ivanovich.'

'But your throat's still sore, I'll bet?'

Kostya nodded, following his grey, shrouded eyes.

'And your ears are still bad, are they?'

'Yes, Ivan Ivanovich.'

The doctor leant forwards, and Kostya heard him muttering to himself as he inspected the hot, stinging skin where the fluid had passed.

'Ivan Ivanovich?' he asked. 'When is my mama coming to see me?'

'You're a brave boy, Konstantin.' Ivan Ivanovich sat back in the chair, twisting the horns of his moustache. He frowned. 'Well . . . Your mother comes here every morning. She brings you a letter and she asks how you are. You know that, don't you? The trouble is, scarlet fever is a very nasty illness and if she comes into your room then she might catch it too.'

'Then . . . how come you can come and see me?'

'I had it when I was a boy, old chap. You can only have it once, you see.'

'Then when is my father coming to see me?'

'Your father's gone to Vyatka.'

Kostya felt his head weigh on to the pillow. His thoughts were so muddled that he began to feel dizzy.

'So . . . When can my mama come and see me, then?'

'It will be a little while yet, I'm afraid. It would be very dangerous for her, just at the moment . . . But if you're good and you keep yourself warm then your brothers and sisters might be able to come and see you a bit sooner. Your mother says that you and your brother Ignat are best friends. Is that right?'

Kostya nodded. He ached with disappointment.

'It's a very serious thing that's happened to you, old fellow . . .' said the doctor, after a moment. 'You've got a lot to cope with. I'll help you as much as I can . . .'

'Ivan Ivanovich?' asked Kostya.

'Yes?'

'Is it New Year's Day?'

'No, old chap.' He smiled, briefly. 'New Year was four days ago now.'

*

When the watchman opened the shutters the following morning, Kostya already had his twenty kopecks sitting on his tongue. All night long he had stayed warm, like he was told, and he wrapped himself meticulously in his blanket before climbing on to his knees and addressing himself to the catch of the inside window, which today was patterned with ferns and flowers of its own. The ice on the outside window was so thick that Kostya had to heat the coin twice before the imperial insignia appeared on the glass and he was able to peep out into the yard and the street, where the Sun filled the faces of the fine stone houses – their walls pink, yellow and the same pale blue as the sky.

With his second hole in place, Kostya began his vigil, his elbows on the sill, alert for any movement in the corridor. He ducked instinctively when he saw Ivan Ivanovich returning from some early assignment, tall and proud in his wolfskin coat and hat, but otherwise he simply watched the brilliant people who passed in Myasnitskaya Street, smothered in so many layers of fur and fleece that they were barely recognizable as people at all. There was a one-legged man in rags he must have been collecting over years – adding each in turn to his outfit. There was a blind man in red velvet trousers, lifting his hat at the prompting of an infant who led him with a stick. There were horses towing bundles of birch trees, like enormous brooms, and ox-carts piled with hay, and then, just as Kostya's neck was beginning to ache, there was a small, slim woman who turned off the street into the chimney-lined shadow in the hospital yard.

Maria Ivanovna wore her best black dress and her mother's bell-shaped cloak. She had a scarf, which encircled her neck and covered the back of her hair. As she passed through the gates, the shadow rose from her boots to her gloves, but her face remained in the startling sunlight, her skin as pale as her high lace collar. A line marred her forehead, but her poise was as perfect as her complexion. Never in his life had Kostya seen so much as a blemish on his mother's smooth, carved cheeks.

'Mama!' He broke the silence, hammering his fists against the window frame, scratching at the fresh ice forming in his eyeholes. 'Mama! Mama!'

Out in the yard, Maria Ivanovna paused, peering through the light, and a second line appeared on her forehead. She looked from the upstairs floor of the hospital to the front door, and then, with a visible intake of breath, she noticed Kostya's two little circles.

'Kostya!' she exclaimed.

Kostya watched as she hurried through the snow, attracting the glances of a couple of peasants who were hauling firewood through a side door. She arrived beneath the window, but she could reach the holes only with her fingertips, and so she fell back a couple of paces – her scarf slipping off her hair, a wash of pink possessing her face.

'Kostya, can you hear me?'

Behind the ice, Kostya was maddened with excitement, dazzled by the sunlight, deafened by the sound of his own voice. He attacked the outside window, but even when he hung from the handle still he couldn't force the catch open, and so he returned to his eyeholes, pressing his face against the glass, and once again he heard her high, bright voice.

'Kostya!'

'Mama!'

'Kostya, I'm so sorry! You're going to get better! We'll make you better, I promise!'

'Mama, I'm better now! Mama! I want to come home!'

*

It was five more days before Ignat sidled into the room, his hair brushed and oiled, his red woollen cap in his hands, his eyes moving from Kostya on his pillow, to the ice-thick window, to the naked, emaciated figure of Saint Vasily on the wall above the bed. To Kostya, who had been visited only by the doctor in the past ten days, his brother looked like a member of some strange, dwarfish species. In Kostya's own old coat and boots, he shuffled across the floorboards and climbed on to the chair – dangling his legs, inspecting his hat.

'Hello, Ignat,' said Kostya, finally.

Ignat glanced up at him, but said nothing.

Words came pouring from Kostya's mouth. 'Oh, Ignat, you wouldn't believe how boring it is here! There's nothing to do, and no one to talk to, and Ivan Ivanovich has even taken my twenty kopecks because I was using it to melt the ice to see outside, and he says I'll catch cold and get ill again, and now I can't even look out of the window!'

'Well . . .' said Ignat. 'That's not fair!'

'That's what I said!'

'What?'

'That's what I said. It's not fair . . .'

Ignat frowned and narrowed his blue eyes. He spoke slowly, hesitantly. 'Well. You have had a very bad illness, Kostya. Anna says that Doctor Lesovsky told Mama that one night he thought you were actually going to die!'

'Really?' asked Kostya.

'Really!'

'So, how is Mama?' Kostya continued. 'Where have you been staying? Has Papa got to Vyatka yet? Has he sent us a tele-gram?'

'Kostya?' said Ignat.

'Yes?'

'Is it true you saw a wolf?'

'What?'

'You told me you saw a wolf. In the night. Just before you got ill . . .'

Kostya looked down at the bedspread, the scattered letters from his mother, the grubby pages of Afanasyev's *Tales*.

Ignat prodded him on the arm. 'Oy!' he said. 'Wake up, you!'

'Sorry,' said Kostya. 'I . . .'

'Well?'

'Well?'

'I asked you if you made it up.'

'No! No, it's true!'

Ignat frowned. He looked at Kostya suspiciously, then he began to rub his chin and his mouth with his hands, as if cover-ing a yawn.

'It is!' Kostya insisted.

Ignat removed his hands. 'How come it didn't eat you, then?'

'I thought it would! It was standing right in the middle of the track, but it had just caught a hare so I . . . I . . .'

Once again Ignat covered his mouth, but this time he appeared to be eating, uttering a series of low, guttural notes.

Around them, it seemed, the hospital had been abandoned. Its patients, its servants, its feldshers, all had descended into silence.

'What?' said Kostya, his voice rising with alarm. 'What are you doing?'

Ignat put his hands on his lap, blinking uncertainly.

'You really can't hear me, Kostya, can you?' he asked, at last.

February 1868

They had already changed horses once, at Boriskovo, when the first light seeped into the February sky. Beneath the leather apron and the thick blankets of the kibitka, Kostya lay with his head on his mother's shoulder and watched the birch trees outside the hood, sweeping the clouds with their fine black branches. To either side of them, his three brothers and four sisters were squeezed together on the fresh straw, their smell warm and familiar above the hot, dirty stink of the horses. The big sledge was rolling, shuddering over ruts and rough log bridges, and Kostya clung tightly to his mother's cloak-cushioned hip and her hard, slightly rounded belly – his ear pressed to the delicate skin beneath her chin, where he could hear her voice without even looking at her face.

'Did you see the little red squirrel, Fekla? . . . That's it. Right up there . . . You know the story about the fox, the hare and the squirrel, don't you? . . . Yes, you do!'

They stopped for breakfast at a hut so deep in the forest that it ought to have had chicken's legs. Extracting himself from the blankets, Kostya watched his mother climb down to the ground, straighten her grey fox-fur hat, retrieve the 'order for horses' from a pocket in her skirts and knock on the door. He looked down a track pristine from the previous night's fall, framed by birches feathered in white, and as a breeze fled among the tree-tops he saw avalanches spilling from the branches, each one feeding the next until the trees appeared to be shivering. He heard the soft, rushing sound of the snow. He turned to find a dog spinning across the yard, and when he saw its champing jaw he heard its bark, and when he saw its flapping tail the bark became a greeting.

In the hot, filthy kitchen of the post-house, Maria Ivanovna and her children sat in a line along a bench and the shelf on the side of the stove. At the table, the Jewish postmaster in his long striped coat was smoking a clay pipe, arguing vigorously with a bear-shaped driver with a mass of curling black hair. The smoke in the room stung Kostya's eyes. At the stove, a bundle of shawls concealed an old woman who was coughing convulsively as she shuffled between an empty saucepan and a pot of cabbage soup. Without a glance, she received their slab of frozen porridge, lopped off a lump with the hatchet from the woodpile, dropped it into a saucepan and turned her attention to the samovar.

On the wall beside the door, there was a tariff of the meals that the old woman was apparently willing to prepare.

'"Veal cutlets",' read Kostya, slowly. '"Sturgeon patties with sour cream. Roast grouse with salted cucumbers. Chicken à la Pojarsky . . ."' He turned to his mother. 'Mama, what's a cutlet?'

'It's a piece of meat,' said Maria Ivanovna. Looking him straight in the face, her voice was light and clear above the room's churning murmur.

'And what's a veal?'

It was only those people Kostya had known before he was ill who still possessed their normal voices. To understand new people, he either had to put his ear close to their mouth or else watch their lips and their eyes and decipher their meaning that way, which was tricky. Animals were different. They made their noises very much as ever, although even with them he was aware that he helped somehow to conjure them into existence. He could stand in front of a bellowing cow, close his eyes and consign it at once to a distant meadow. With his eyes closed, there was little to complicate the silence. Here in the post-house, there was the clack of his teeth as he chewed his bread. There was the gurgle as his tea drained through the sugar lump in his cheek. There were voices, but they were vague, meaningful only in moments. He might have been sitting outside in the forest, listening to these people through the muffling snow, the breeze and the thick wooden walls.

*

Maria Ivanovna made no objection when, after breakfast, Kostya left his family to clamber back into the kibitka and himself climbed up on to the bench beside the bear-shaped driver, who sat a small, crumpled hat on his head, gathered the six reins of the three fresh horses, struck the central mare with his short whip and set out north-east at the gallop of a cavalry officer under fire. Ten minutes earlier, a peasant with an ox-cart had come plodding past the post-house, but the driver overtook him in a matter of moments, shouting in a thunderclap voice that even Kostya could make out. When the horses hit the untouched snow, he felt the excitement of Vrangel in the Arctic. He clung to his seat and squinted against the flying snow and the freezing wind, while the horses poured steam like a locomotive and the bell in the arch between the shafts danced and told the forest, the long straight track and any other peasants unwise enough not to have collected sufficient firewood back in the autumn that this was a post-sledge and would be travelling at speed.

'Fast enough?' yelled the driver, his breath a gale of garlic.

'No!' said Kostya.

'No?!' The driver's eyes goggled above cheeks scored with little blood vessels. He set about the peripheral horses with his whip. 'Come on, my little doves! Faster! Faster!'

The team was running now *ventre à terre*, the muscles flickering beneath their thick winter coats. On his bench, the driver sat as easily as he had sat on his chair in the post-house, and he continued to talk – although Kostya caught only an occasional word. The boy let his eyes run across the rippling silver of the birch forest. There were patches of blue in the narrow sky above the track. The light was growing, diluting the shadows. He saw thin trunks bowed into arches by the weight of the snow, snakes of snow that hung from the branches to the ground and fat snow piles that looked so much like cows or old women it seemed inconceivable that somebody hadn't come out here to sculpt them.

'Hi!' The driver prodded his shoulder, leant towards him, spoke again.

Kostya started. 'Sorry . . . It's my hearing.'

'Ah! I thought . . .' The driver tapped his head significantly and continued in a great bass roar. 'Can you hear me now?'

Kostya nodded. Such was the stench that, even at this speed, he had to look away to breathe.

'Where are you going?'

'Vyatka,' said Kostya.

'The devil! Why do you want to go there?'

'It's where my uncle lives. My father's gone there to work.'

The driver looked at him as if he were a lunatic. 'Vyatka's the ends of the Earth! They send criminals there as a punishment!'

'I know . . .'

'Where are you staying tonight, then?'

'Mama says she wants to go straight to Nizhny Novgorod.'

'Nizhegorod, ho!' The driver gave a war cry, and attended to his whip.

Without warning, the horses burst from the forest into a clearing that straddled an Oka two or three times wider than

Kostya had seen on any excursion from Ryazan. Beneath the mottled sky, between the blue-tinged shores of the standing trees, the snow rolled and surged across the wreckage of felling – revealing in places bushes, stumps and branches like the arms of drowning men. Above the pointed ears and whirling manes of the horses, the track vanished over the bank and, a moment later, the kibitka plummeted and arrived on the ice, where the scars of feet, hooves, paws and sledges converged to the north. A misshapen thatched hut watched them from a prominence, straw plugging the broken panes in its windows, smoke struggling from a black hole in its white roof. The children who had emerged at the sound of the whip and the bell were beaming and waving from the door – their hands concealed in the sleeves of their too-big coats.

*

For the last two hours of the afternoon, the Sun wheeled through the trees around the track: a bloodshot eye following their progress, now staring straight down the long pink ruts behind them, now sliding among the pines and the birches so that their branches sparkled orange, violet, gold. They passed through villages of low, dishevelled houses and fat wooden churches whose three-barred crosses leant towards the north. They passed through Melenki, Selino and, as the Sun set entirely, they passed through Murom – its crenellations and hourglass cupolas picked black out of the crimson sky.

In the night, Kostya lay against the cold wooden wall of the kibitka. Beside him, the voices and faces of the others were lost to the darkness, and so, little by little, he pulled himself around the corner of the apron, out of the hood, and curled between the overlapping planks and Ignat's bony legs, his hat pulled down over his eyebrows and the blankets covering his nose.

Silent, unmoving above the shivering sledge, the stars hung untroubled by clouds or even the moisture that flooded the air on those summers' nights when he might sleep outside on the grass. Kostya followed the track that lay above their own, conscribed by the treetops. He imagined that the stars were the atoms of some monumental being, perhaps of God Himself. He imagined that he was flying through the ether, pulled not by horses but by a skein of swans, and that soon he would arrive on other planets circling other stars, where he would be hailed tsar by creatures who communicated not, he thought, by sound but by means of pictures mounted on their chests, which they would use to send messages even faster than the telegraph.

They were some versts north of Novoselki when Kostya felt a change in the movement of the horses. Lifting his head, he saw the driver's pistol ignite the bare, louring trees – accompanied by the first proper sound that he had heard since sunset. He saw in the light of the stars and a rising slice of Moon the horses fighting against their traces, the bell between the shafts thrashing as if possessed. On his bench, the driver appeared to be shouting. In silhouette, he aimed again and a plume of fire exploded into the darkness, where, as he blinked away the lights, Kostya saw a shadow flitting across the snow, weightless as mist. It was impossible to tell the size of the wolf. It could have been four arshins away, or twenty, but as the driver fired a third time he saw that there were others – some of them weaving effortlessly through the trees around them, some so close that they seemed to be dodging the horses' hoofs.

It was only with the driver's fourth shot that one of the shadows tripped and tumbled, suddenly substantial, and at once the others disappeared. Frantically, the driver threw his whip out over the horses' backs, fumbling in his pockets for more bullets. Kostya looked among the Moon-coloured trunks of the birch trees. He leant over the side of the kibitka and, beyond the hood where his mother was waving and beckoning to him, he saw the wolves swarming on the body of their fallen comrade – the first of them already returning to the chase, gaining on them steadily, a bore of black against the snow.

As he looked back towards the driver, Kostya saw the left horse stumble. It recovered at once, throwing its head against the harness, but plainly the wolves had not missed the movement. When the driver fired again, not one of them fell back for the body. Instead they closed on the tiring mare, condensing as a pack, lunging at her Moon-cut ribs like the waves against the sides of a steamboat, while Kostya wondered what would happen if the horse were to fall and meet the kibitka at this furious speed, how it would feel to be catapulted through the air, to be torn apart by those long, arching teeth.

*

It was late the following morning when Nizhny Novgorod appeared above the east bank of the Oka, its walls and domes alight in the low winter sunshine, white and gold as the celestial city in the stories. Buried among her children, Maria Ivanovna pointed past the edge of the hood, past the grand expanse of ice, the tracks of the sledges, the fires and the fishermen – her other arm tight around Kostya's waist, her lips set almost to his ear.

'There!' Her eyes widened. 'You see that clutch of pine trees in the forest, poking above the firs and birches? The black ones, Kostya, do you see? They call those Savelov's Mane.' Mysteriously, she laughed and her jaw seemed to quiver. 'The woods here all belong to Count Shuvalov. He's Chief of the Tsar's Gendarmes these days, but even back then he was always in Petersburg, being important, so in the autumn my cousins and

I would come down here with axes and ropes. We collected all the firewood like that, and old Count Shuvalov none the wiser!'

She turned to look at Ignat.

'Well . . .' She bit her lip a little guiltily. 'It was only dead wood, Ignat. He didn't want it. And everyone else in Kunavino got their firewood in just the same way.'

'What else did you do in Nizhny, Mama?' asked Kostya.

'Well, Little Bird, I attended the gymnasium for a whole year, so I did lots of things – although mostly I studied Latin and mathematics, and learnt the catechism, which was very, very boring . . .'

'How old were you?'

'In '47, I was . . . fifteen years old.' The sledge turned and the sunlight hit her full in the face, her silver hairs shining like the snow. There was a darkness beneath her eyes that might have been drawn there with ink. 'Good Lord, it was twenty-one years ago! I was younger than you, Alyosha! And you, Mitya! Except for a couple of visits to Ryazan, it was the first time I'd ever been further than Pronsk. I remember . . .' She looked at the fields beneath Count Shuvalov's wood. 'I remember, in the spring, in the mornings before school we would come running down that hill to pick mushrooms. Oh, it was magic! There were daisies and buttercups and primroses and forget-me-nots, and dew on the grass, and the mist on the river, and the Sun just rising over the Dyatlov Hills!'

*

The post-house in Nizhny Novgorod was two streets from the docks, the size of a warehouse, maintained at the temperature of an oven by an ingenious system of iron pipes. In the corridors and the stairwell, men, women and families as sprawling as their own pressed between the rooms and the street. Girls carried precarious pans of boiling water and misshapen loaves of black bread whose sour smell filled the stuffy air. The place looked noisy. Everyone Kostya saw seemed to be shouting to someone on the far side of the crowd, and even when he, his mother, his three brothers and four sisters found their own room and set down their trunk he could still feel the movement on the floorboards above them and outside the door: a constant vibration, as though the building were an enormous musical instrument.

The room was small, filthy and lit by one high window, which revealed a few straggling clouds. It contained a table, a jug of hot water, a pockmarked mirror, an icon of St John the Baptist, two bare beds and an inordinate number of cockroaches rifling in the dust with their fishing-rod antennae. Next to the door hung the same meaningless menu that they had seen in the post-house the previous morning, together with a notice indicating that it was 351 versts to Ryazan, 454 versts to Vyatka, 431 versts to Moscow, 958 versts to St Petersburg and 6,430 versts to Vladivostok – a journey, Kostya calculated, that would take them very nearly a month.

'Food's ready, Kostya,' said Maria Ivanovna, crouching in front of him. 'Are you hungry?'

Kostya noticed the smell of thawing porridge.

'Six thousand four hundred and thirty versts away!' he replied, in amazement.

'What is?'

'Vladivostok!'

'It's a long old way.'

'It would take us twenty-seven days to get there. Unless we travelled all night as well.'

His mother smiled and kissed him on the forehead. 'Well, Mr Explorer, if I can drag you from your sums we are going to have some lunch, then we are going to climb the hill to the kremlin.'

The street behind the post-house was deep and grey, the snow so worn by wheels and runners that the cobblestones were almost bare. Among the traffic, twenty or more young men and boys in thin grey uniforms, eyes lowered, rode on a pair of big sledges. They had been shaved of half of their beards and hair, so that their exposed heads resembled skulls. They wore chains on their ankles and held their arms tight around their narrow chests. The iron-clad runners threw sparks from the stones. The family wove between steam-snorting horses, past a shop whose windows displayed every colour of cloth you could imagine: orange, pink, turquoise, dandelion yellow. Anna had to tuck Masha beneath her arm to make her come away. Leaving an alleyway spattered with the dirty ice of washerwomen, they arrived in a ravine, its sides striped with compost where lean dogs nosed disconsolately. Above them, there were lime trees furry with lichen and a house so grand and pale that it might have been made out of marzipan.

In a square halfway up the hill, Kostya sat down on a packing case and watched his mother shepherd the others among the bales of wool, the sheepskins, hemp ropes, felt boots and harnesses piled outside the shops. His thin legs shivered. Beside him, a couple of merchants were smoking, spitting into the snow, talking indecipherably.

'Tired, are you, Kostyusha?' Anna appeared in front of him, smiling with his own dark eyes and the domed forehead of their father.

'No!'

'Yes, you are!'

She took him by the shoulders and swung him on to her back, and when he happened to touch his sister's throat he found that he could hear her fairly well. He let his head hang forwards and the street smells of pies, birch smoke and hemp-seed oil met the juniper smell in her long black hair.

'Anya?' he asked. 'Who were the men in the sledges?'

'The prisoners?' said Anna. 'Poles, little brother. Off to Vyatka, just like us!'

'Why?'

'Well, maybe they're going to Siberia, I don't know . . .'

They were climbing through an arcade of shoe shops and tailors, strewn with straw and splinters of wood, thick with crowds and sledges.

'Why, though?'

'Oh!' Kostya felt his sister's voice box jump beneath his fingers and she turned half-circle so that he could see the open door of a workshop where men were building furniture with an arsenal of tools, their ceiling hung with special glass balls that filled the room with daylight. 'Just imagine the things you could make with that lot, hey?'

Although Kostya had heard plenty of stories from his mother about crystal mountains and cloud-veiled Circassian peaks, he had never before seen anything like the hill in Nizhny Novgorod. It was taller than the pines of Savelov's Mane, taller by far than Uspensky Cathedral and the bank of the Trubezh put together, and as its crown it wore a kremlin so magnificent that it was surely the finest in the world.

When Anna set Kostya back on the ground, he stood beneath a giant, whitewashed tower with a roof like a sorcerer's hat and looked down a tobogganing slope of suicidal steepness towards a church of golden domes, the snowy warehouses and entombed barges that lay along the docks. Beyond them, the Volga was a frozen infinity where men and horses moved in miniature beneath the enormous, cloud-scratched sky. To the left, the little Oka arrived like some poor cousin from the south, dividing the city from the squares, the enclosures, the fire-breaks, fire-towers, churches and canals of the Makaryev Fair – in summer, the most important event in all Russia. On the head of the peninsula rose the half-completed roofs of a cathedral. Among the distant fields ran a tiny pair of parallel lines, and even as Kostya watched the Moscow train was leaving the station: the easternmost terminus of the entire railway system.

Kostya moved to the brink of the slope. He strained his ears, peered through the tumult of smoke and steam.

'Ignat?' he asked at last, turning to his brother. 'What kind of engine was it? Could you hear the whistle?'

March 1868

Even in the hour before dawn, the lanterns continued to burn on Tsarevo-Konstantinovskaya Church and Holy Trinity Cathedral: tiny, tentative lights, tracing baroque shapes against the black sky. From the kitchen window of the new apartment, Kostya could see their contours clearly above the snow-rounded roofs across the street. The cathedral stood on one of Vyatka's seven low hills, and although a few of the lanterns had died during the night there still were the eaves and the roofline of the refectory, and the ledges of the bell tower, and even the tip of the spire. Tsarevo-Konstantinovskaya Church was closer, and its tower stood plainly on the western side of Tsarevskaya Street. Its parapets hung like marshalled stars. It was astonishing that, on his tour of the city, the mayor had managed to assemble so much tallow. It was astonishing that anyone could have scaled those walls and straddled those ridges.

A volley of firecrackers greeted the first impression of dawn. A rocket arched above the roofs and left a burning trail, which Kostya could still see inside his eyelids several minutes later. Slowly, like a drawing of Orion or the Centaur, the cathedral materialized within its constellation. Its spire shaded in the blackness beneath the crowning light. The east wall of the pillar-carved tower came apart from its silhouette. To the south, one of the two dark apertures in the tower of Tsarevo-Konstantinovskaya Church began to blink – grey, grey, grey – until at last Kostya was able to see the swinging bells among the failing lanterns and the peeling whitewash, and behind them the bell-ringers, working their ropes with hands and feet, their movement a music in itself.

*

It was still scarcely daylight when Kostya felt footsteps on the stairs, and his mother, Anna, Alexei and Dmitri erupted into the kitchen in a gale of night-time air, red cheeks, long coats and woolly hats. They were singing so raucously that he could tell their song at once:

> *Easter eggs! Easter eggs!*
> *Give them to the man who begs!*
> *For Christ is risen from the dead . . .*

'Christ is risen!' exclaimed Maria Ivanovna.

'Truly He is risen!' Kostya replied, hurrying across the room from the open shutter.

His mother bent down and kissed him three times with great formality.

'Little Bird,' she said. 'What are you doing awake at this hour?'

'I was hungry, Mama!'

'Hungry?' Her eyes shone. 'Well, I think we can do something about that!'

One by one, Kostya stretched to kiss the others – his brothers' faces prickling his cheeks – then, as they sat down to remove their boots, apparently bemoaning the lack of chairs in church, he went to fetch the jug of pussy-willow branches that he and Ignat had gathered the previous afternoon. He set it carefully in the middle of the table, among the eggs that they had all dyed red on Holy Thursday, the frosted Easter bread and the pyramid of *pascha* whose sweet cheese smell had woken him in the first place.

All of the children were gathered round the table, ogling the Easter breakfast and presenting themselves to one another to be kissed, when Eduard Ignatyevich appeared in the door of the bedroom that he now shared with his four sons. Broad and dark in his heavy black jacket, he hooked his spectacles over his ears and went to the window to survey the crowds of worshippers still returning from church, their lanterns blazing in the half-light. A Catholic in name, born into the numerous nobility of eastern Poland, Eduard Ignatyevich had never been seen to enter a church of any kind. He took his cigarette case from his pocket and struck a match, and as he coughed and steadied himself against the yellowing wallpaper he inspected a bead of water which was dangling from an icicle on the eaves – sparkling with a hundred tiny lanterns.

Finally, he fastened the top button of his shirt and went to sit at the head of the table, opposite his wife, who was waiting to bless the meal. He spoke, but his lips and face were concealed by his black moustache and his grey-patterned beard and Kostya could understand not a word.

*

The family kept to the pavement as they walked the few hundred arshins to Sobornaya Square, where women drove ox-carts festooned with every scrap of colour that they possessed, and men in golden caps and bell-bottom trousers crossed themselves as yet another procession carried its icon between jubilant households. Among the stalls, the air was ripe with honey-cake and roasted nuts. Kostya saw glass eggs containing miniature wax roses and angels. He saw flurries of colour as siskins and goldfinches were released from their winter cages and rose to join the sparrows and starlings in the pallid sky. On Kazanskaya Street, he ran his fingers along the cast-iron railings that led to the stucco gatehouse of the Alexandrovsky Gardens, where sledge-drivers were guarding their upholstery from the sticky hands of inquisitive children, and he noticed the sledge of his Uncle Stanislaw: a sleek, red-trimmed vehicle, its two black horses adorned with scarlet ribbons, harnessed in single file in the manner peculiar to Vyatka.

Kostya heard the band before he saw them. He stopped in the path and frowned, listening to some lumbering, low-pitched instrument.

'Mama!' he exclaimed. 'Music!'

Despite her best black dress, which she could still just fasten around her belly, Maria Ivanovna crouched down in the wet sand and threw her arms around his neck. She planted so many kisses on his lips and cheeks that he had to wipe his face on the sleeve of his sheepskin.

'You see!' She beamed at him. 'What did I tell you? I don't care what the doctors say. You're going to get better! You are!'

She grasped his hand and as they passed along the tall, wooded bank, where a brass band was playing in neat, frogged uniforms, through a luminous mist Kostya saw that the Vyatka River had dissolved into a multitude of icebergs.

'Mama!' He tugged on her arm. 'Can I go down and see the ice? Please, Mama! Please!'

'Little Bird!' Maria Ivanovna smiled, patiently. 'We are going to see your cousins. We're going on the swings! You want to go on the swings, don't you?'

Kostya admitted that he did.

'Well, then,' she said. 'I'm sure the ice will still be there this afternoon.'

On the central lawns, every manner of person was assembled. There were bare-cheeked gentlemen and ladies in crinoline and ankle-length cloaks. There were peasants with bound legs, bast shoes and bottles of spirit. There were children cutting the year's first mudslides. There were couples on the courting swings: a series of planks suspended from a single pole, which they propelled by standing one at each end, thrusting themselves backwards and forwards as they attempted to 'go around the top'. And above them all rose the Easter swings, erected back in early February for the extravagances of Butter Week – their covers removed, their gaily painted boats sailing in the warm spring air.

'Can you hear the song, Kostya?' asked Maria Ivanovna, keenly. 'Can you hear what they're singing?'

Kostya shook his head.

His mother hesitated, obviously disappointed, then she put her lips to his ear and sang in her high, hymnal voice:

> *Our swing is swinging*
> *From its seven straight poles.*
> *We sit in our cradle*
> *And we sing out our souls.*
> *And the higher we swing,*
> *Or so I have been told,*
> *The higher our flax*
> *Pushes out of the mould!*

Stanislaw Ignatyevich Tsiolkovsky was a man so fat that he could sit with his hands on top of his belly, like a woman expecting a baby. He had a beard dyed black, a suit with waist-coat and watch-chain, and a raccoon-skin coat the size of a tent. Squeezed beside him on the wrought-iron bench, his sturdy wife and daughters wore ruffles of pink, and his fair-haired, ten-year-old son, Tomasz, wore clothes identical to his own in every particular – down to the white chamois gloves.

Kostya felt his mother remove her hand as she and his father went to exchange the Easter kiss with his aunt and uncle. He saw his sister Anna produce the bundle of *pascha* and Easter bread that they had left over from breakfast, while his uncle's maid spread a rubber sheet across the ground and opened a hamper to reveal bacon, cheese, milk, bread, wine, brightly painted eggs, and pies still steaming from the oven. In his sheepskin jacket and his darned linen trousers, Kostya felt the colour coming to his face and he turned away quickly towards the six mighty swings – the men leaning backwards to heave on their ropes, the women clinging to their Easter bonnets, the children holding their arms like wings.

*

It must have been warm in the hills to the south of Vyatka. By the time that Kostya, Ignat and Tomasz came slithering down the path to the river that afternoon the water had swallowed the islands beneath Trifonov Monastery. Icebergs were pouring towards the north, carrying bushes, hayricks and whole trees. On one, a dog was sitting upright, like an interested passenger. It was usual on these late March days for the temperature to rise above freezing in the morning and to fall again sharply in the afternoon, but today the clouds were low and thick. The breeze possessed none of its customary bite. It brought gulls in crowds, diving with folded wings, barely able to reach the banks for the weight of the fish in their beaks.

As Kostya passed the warehouses and the big hotel, he watched the men on the beach across the river at Dymkovo, crossing themselves as they launched shallow boats with heavy gunwales and, when any gap presented itself, paddled frantically for the Easter festivities. Sometimes the boats would get trapped in the floes and vanish north around Simonovsky Island. Sometimes they would reach one of the wharfs, where the barges and the city's two resident steamboats still wore skirts of ice, and their passengers would jump ashore, gesticulate wildly to the little figures they had left behind and hurry away into Razderikhinsky ravine.

'Steamboats are nowhere near as good as steam engines,' declared Kostya, striding along the path, a step ahead of his brother and cousin. 'In England there's a train that goes at 123 versts per hour! A 4-2-4. A hundred and twenty-three versts! Imagine! You could leave Vyatka and reach Moscow in seven hours. I'd like to see a steamboat travel as fast as that!'

He paused, decided that Tomasz would probably raise the subject of engine power, and waited, as if listening.

'Well,' he conceded, 'it's true that steamships do have much larger engines. Back in Ryazan, we would see some monster steamships, but that's because the river there is so much bigger than it is here.' He glanced at the Vyatka, which was, conservatively, the width of the Oka at Nizhny Novgorod. 'I read a book about steamships, so I know all about them. Did you know that the SS *Great Eastern* has engines that make 8,300 horsepower? It has ten whole boilers and a hundred furnaces!'

It was not until they reached the goods sheds next to the steamboat *Kama* that Kostya was able to turn to face the others. To his relief, he found that neither of them was speaking, and so, cursing his father for forcing them to bring their cousin, he tugged down the hem of his old coat and went to sit on the steep muddy bank, looking past his boots at the eddying icebergs.

'I said,' said Tomasz, putting his perfumed lips to Kostya's ear, 'do you know what we do?'

'What's that?'

'We go jumping on the ice. I bet you don't do that in Ryazan!'

Kostya smiled tolerantly. 'Jumping on the ice? Of course we do.'

'No need to shout, *mon cousin*!' said Tomasz. He laughed, the soft flesh quivering between his chin and his black bow tie.

'What?' Kostya demanded. 'What's so funny?'

'Oh, I was just imagining you crossing the ice!' He laughed again. 'You with your mother, holding your hand! "Come on, Kostya, darling. Big leap now! That's it!"'

Kostya stared at him in amazement. He opened his mouth, running back through the words that he was sure he had understood, but still he could come to no other meaning. Furiously, he jumped to his feet and glared into his cousin's pleased pink face, then he slid straight down the slippery clay and hopped on to the nearest iceberg.

'Come on, then!' he screamed. 'I'd like to see you try it!'

Tomasz looked down the slope and his cheeks lost colour. Beside him, Ignat was waving and shouting, but Kostya turned deliberately and jumped across the next stretch of brown, slushy water. To demonstrate his contempt, he didn't even look to see if his cousin was following him and instead made a couple more well-timed leaps to a spot where he could consider the twin decks, the white paddle wheels and the black-ringed funnel of the *Kama* – a fisherman on the prow, smashing the head of a perch against a railing.

'Oh! Careful!' Kostya turned to see Tomasz step uncertainly on to a berg near the bank, his eyes on his well-spread, patent-leather boots. 'I think you might be a bit too heavy for that one!'

Tomasz shouted something.

'You'll have to catch me first!'

Again Kostya ignored Ignat's gestures. He took another leap and came to the edge of the eddy, where the bergs were revolving slowly, and when he stood still he found himself presented in turn with the gilded cupolas of Feodorovskaya Church, the leafless woods around the Alexandrovsky Gardens, the needle spires and bellying domes of Pyatnitsky Church and Holy Trinity Cathedral, which rose above the tall, bare bank. Kostya held his arms out at either side. He knew that Tomasz could arrive at any moment, but still he watched the ice to the south become the still-snowy meadows, the hull-sliced beach at Dymkovo and the sawmill near Simonovsky Island, where the gulls fell like snowflakes and a boatload of would-be revellers was scrambling wearily ashore.

When the iceberg turned full circle, Kostya could see no trace of his cousin. He looked back at the river to check if he had been outflanked, then up at the path, and finally at his brother, who was skidding down the bank, gesturing more frantically than ever. Beneath him, suddenly, Tomasz came yawning to the surface, his tongue red, his pale hair slick across his eyes. He seemed to scream as he sank, his white gloves waving from a white-fringed wave, and Kostya began to jump across the ice towards him. Arriving on the nearest berg, he fell to his knees. He saw Tomasz rise again in the dark water and managed to grab his collar, but then his cousin found the broken edge of the ice and tried to heave himself upwards, and although Kostya threw himself backwards the ice was wet and sinking, and he was no match for the weight of that coat.

Like most of his friends in Ryazan, Kostya had never learnt to swim. The water was shallow by the beach on the Trubezh, and even on those hot days in July and August when the Oka was crowded with diving, splashing boys he had never ventured out of his depth. Plunging head first into the Vyatka, missing his cousin by a tochka, he could find no trace of either the surface or the bottom. The water was so cold that his skull seemed to be contracting on his brain. He gasped and his mouth filled with water. He flailed his limbs, but it was as if he were suspended by some invisible peg, unable to move in any direction. Through the terrible blackness, he saw a dim, grey pattern, like a window in the winter, and as he tried to pull himself towards it so he met the slippery underside of the ice. Desperately, he scrabbled for a finger hold. He felt an arm graze his face, and a hand, but then a pain like a needle thrust deep into his belly and he sank back into the blackness – the stars coming out around him, as they would on any clear evening.

When Ignat dragged him back on to the iceberg, Kostya hardly shivered for the cold. Distantly, he could hear himself coughing. He could see his brother's face, flushed and averted beneath his red woollen hat, the sleeves of his sheepskin sodden to the shoulders. He could see Tomasz crawling back up the bank with neither coat nor hat, dripping, stumbling away along the path, and although he had no strength to speak, still, in little gasps, he vomited egg, sausage, bacon, beef pie, tea, cottage cheese and Easter bread – which found the grooves of runners in the shelving ice and made a molten island on the dirty water.

May 1868

The city that emerged from beneath the snow was small and dilapidated: a city only in name. Six months of soot caked the walls and roofs of the gymnasium, the library, the prison, the F. Veretennikov bank, the P. Klobukov department store, the dye-works belonging to Stanislaw Ignatyevich, the college of technology and agriculture where Eduard Ignatyevich taught mathematics and natural history. The rutted streets reeked with the excrement of humans, dogs and horses, so that even the peasants walked with rags held to their Sun-pink faces. Hooves and wheels threw waves of slime against the wooden houses that framed the city centre, and in these bleak northerly regions where the farming season lasted barely four and a half months few people found time to clean their gables and windows, which may privately have been red, green, blue, yellow, intricate and attractive.

Only the churches rose above the squalor. As he followed his mother through the holiday crowds, Kostya passed Tsarevo-Konstantinovskaya Church, Pokrovsky Church, Pyatnitsky Church, the Church of the Holy Transfiguration – their pale towers faint through the thin May rain. He passed Spassky Cathedral, Holy Resurrection Cathedral and, greatest of all, Holy Trinity Cathedral, whose dome appeared to echo the sky. It was here, so his mother had told him, that the priests kept the miracle-working icon of St Nikolai – revealed by God in the village of Velikoretsky, far to the north, where it was returned every year in a procession famous throughout Russia. The two of them paused beneath its snow-white walls, its airy windows and stucco fans. They crossed themselves before they turned towards the river.

*

On the floating bridge across the Vyatka, the rain shone from the rippling boards, the wandering handrails, the beards, the cloaks, the staffs, the packs, the haltered calves and sheep whose cries rose like commands above the joyous, inchoate voices. It released smells of smoke, sweat and, faintly, the frankincense from the cathedral. It made the procession seem indivisible: a single, grey-brown body that fed from the city, over the river, on to the broad floodplain.

In Dymkovo, Kostya looked past the cascading leaves of the birch trees at the openwork carving of the one-room houses, perched above stables where an occasional horse was hiding from the bluebottles. He saw a top-heavy windmill with a long pole protruding from one side, so that the miller could turn the blades to face the wind. He saw fields divided into strips, a third of them bristling with the short green spears of rye and flax, a third of them fallow, blue with cornflowers and yellow with tansy, a third of them naked clay, where those few peasants not in the procession were guiding ploughshares scarcely longer than their fingers – the ribs of their horses straining against their taut, wet hides.

In the forest, men struggled to free their crutches from the hungry mud. Old women shuffled beneath hunched backs, stepping ponderously over the black distorted roots that rose from the trodden ground and the trees that lay flat where the path was wide and divided like a river around the birch saplings and the willow bushes that had sprung up in the uncommon light. Where the path was narrow, the fallen trees leant between the dark walls of the forest so that only one person could pass at a time and the waiting crowds suffered the descent of midges and mosquitoes in numbers even greater than their own.

They had just left the village of Kisela when Maria Ivanovna stepped off the path and sank on to the thin grass beneath a crooked ash, grimacing, wrapping her arms around her waist. She gestured at Kostya with a downwards motion of her flattened right hand, which, in the language of signals that had developed between them over the past few months, could either mean 'sit down', 'slow down' or, sometimes, 'no'. Beneath her red-and-gold kerchief, Maria Ivanovna was breathing rapidly – her eyes closed, her face pulled so tight that the bones might have been chiselled from her colourless cheeks. Between the folds of her rubber cloak, there was a dark grey line on her grey woollen dress, which branched across the ledge of her belly. She had to gesture again before Kostya made a tent from his own cloak, covered their heads and squeezed beneath her arm.

He felt her breathing slow, slowly, saw the determination return to her face, but still several minutes passed before she opened her eyes, removed his boots, wrung out his lumpy woollen socks and swapped them between his feet to help with the rubbing. Summoning her strength, she set her hands on the ground, and Kostya followed her gaze through the curtain of water, past the white, mud-patterned clothes of a group of native Finns, towards a woman in a dun-coloured headscarf who was pulling a man with withered legs on a small wooden wagon – threads of steam rising faintly from the axle.

*

In Bobino that evening, Kostya was tired and cold and hungry and hobbling on feet that had been wet all day. It was his turn to carry the pack and he tramped two steps behind his mother, who herself walked with her head drooping and her arms round her belly, which was discernible only in the weight of her steps. He paid no attention to the huts that lined the central track, whose windows seemed to hide in shame beneath their shaggy roofs. Some of the other pilgrims had dragged branches with them from the forest, and the chill air carried wafts of porridge, eggs, cabbage and resinous smoke. Among the long, tangled shadows of an orchard, they found a patch of grass in the multitude eating, talking and sleeping, kicked aside a few sheep droppings and spread a cloak on the damp ground.

'Kostya?' said Maria Ivanovna, finally.

Kostya sat down beside her, but he looked at the apple trees, their trunks black and contorted against the low Sun, their flowers the same translucent pink as the sky.

'Kostya?' his mother repeated. She was speaking directly into his ear. 'I know what you're thinking, but I'm fine! Really, I am! And I know what your father said, but he's wrong, Kostya! I love him very much, but he's a terrible old cynic and much good it does him! Look at all these people! Look at them! They say that 20,000 of us are going to Velikoretsky this year. That's like the entire population of Ryazan! That's three times more people than even live in Vyatka, so just think how far they must have come to be here! How can they all be wrong, Kostya? How? Go in faith and in sincerity and God will help you! You'll see!'

Kostya turned his eyes to the procession still toiling through the village: side-lit figures of endless variety, weary and muddy as themselves. He watched one old man, his feet bare, his sheepskin covered with rough-stitched patches, and for the first time in his life he found himself wondering what he himself might be like in five years, fifteen years, fifty years' time.

'I know you don't like me worrying over you,' his mother

continued, 'but I can't help it, Little Bird! I'm your mother and you're my son and I'll do anything to help you. Anything!'

Later, in the luminous darkness when the Sun had dropped behind the jagged forest and the sky turned golden as the great domed ceiling in Holy Trinity Cathedral, the temperature fell sharply and Kostya's breath floated in the air. A scattering of stars peeped through the patterns of the clouds, and the villagers, who had earlier dispensed pancakes, sugar, carrots and spirit to the crowds, now descended on the orchard with arms full of brushwood, erected bonfires and waved sheets of birch bark to spread the smoke and protect the delicate blossom from the frost. On the hard ground, where the ice gleamed on the well-chewed grass, Kostya lay inside his mother's coat, the baby stirring faintly against his back, and as they curled closer in the gathering cold, it was difficult to tell which of them was comforting the other.

*

'The Sun, Little Bird,' said Maria Ivanovna, as they lay together on the grass of Monastyrskoe the following night, 'is thirty times bigger than he appears to you and I. He looks so small simply because he is such a long way above the Earth. The Sun is a big, grand character, very fat and very important. He has a crown and a long mink cloak that would be the pride of the tsar himself. Every morning the Lord sends His angels to dress him for the day in golden breeches, a golden jacket and a golden shirt with frills at the neck. Every evening they return to dress him in his nightshirt and his paper nightcap, ready for his bed. The Sun is so fine and so glorious that, by night, the Lord charges His archangels, Gabriel, Michael and Raphael, to stay with him and cover him with their wings. When he rises in the morning, the Sun is flanked by flaming phoenixes and birds of paradise who have first dived into the ocean so that their feathers are wet and they are not scorched by his rays . . .'

Through tremulous eyelids, Kostya watched a girl asleep beside them, a lamb in her arms. He looked through the smoke rising from hundreds of little fires, condensing in a plume above the village's low hill, its gardens full of cabbage and cucumber, the tower of its church black against the fiery sky. He watched the red Sun perched on the dark forest. He felt his mother's lips, warm and soft against his ear, the muscles burning in his legs, and he moved his bare, still-bleeding feet against the cool grass since the night was scarcely less hot than the day.

'There are those,' Maria Ivanovna went on, softly, 'who call the cock a prophet. It is he who wakes, flutters his wings and announces to the world a new day. Every morning he crows three times. Once, to say that the Sun will be resurrected, like Our Lord Jesus Christ was resurrected, like we shall all be resurrected on the Day of Days, as Paul the Apostle has told us. Twice, to ask Our Lord Jesus Christ to grant the Sun his passage through the sky. Three times, to sing that Christ is the Life, *that He achieves all.*

'And this is the story of the Sun, and how he was made by the Lord. Amen.'

*

The crowd that stood by the Great River at Velikoretsky to greet the icon of St Nikolai was larger than Kostya could ever have imagined, and even when he pulled himself on to the branch of a convenient birch tree still he could see no limit to this church whose walls were the woods, whose roof was the black-bottomed clouds. Among the numberless Slavs looking south towards the diagonal of smoke beyond the arch of the river, he saw Finns, Mari and Votyaks, and Tatars, men with round fur caps and the features of Mongols, women with headdresses glistening with coins, people who were pagans, Muslims, not Christians at all, but still stood here with their families, their calves and their sheep, and watched the steam-boat of the Governor of Vyatka emerge from the sky-stretching pines, its paddle wheels seething, its white sides draped with scarlet cloth.

In its wake came every vessel on the Vyatka River. There was the *Vyatka* itself, its twin decks thick with merchants, officials, visiting grandees and nobles returned for the summer from Moscow and St Petersburg. There was the *Kama*. There were sails white in the uneasy sunshine, teams of long, even oars, the dayboats of shopkeepers and the tubs of fishermen, and even before they reached the spring and the birch tree where the icon had been revealed 485 years earlier many of the passengers hurled themselves into the water, scrambling up the bank, crossing themselves and opening their arms to the heavens.

Amid the crying animals and the ululating pilgrims, they climbed the hill towards Velikoretsky Monastery, its blue-gold campanile poking from the biblical dust cloud. Faintly, Kostya heard the clamour of its madly swinging bells. He saw women proffering kopecks, calling out the names of their dead to the boys who sat on every gravestone, writing prayers with pen and ink. He saw an avenue of cripples lining the path to the tall white arch of the monastery gate: a legless man on a ragged little sledge, his arms carved with muscle, his hands like old leather shoes, a girl with no arms at all, just hands that flapped grotesquely from her shoulder blades. At the gate itself, he saw a man with a face so eaten by some hideous disease that his jawbone and blackened teeth lay open to the air, saliva hanging from his chin to a pale smear on the breast of his filthy shirt, and still he shook the copper coins in his tin bowl.

In the courtyard, it suddenly started to hail. An impression of silence came over the army of people pressing towards the Cathedral of the Transfiguration to meet the miracle-working icon, and to escape the big, stinging stones Kostya and his mother covered their heads with their cloaks and gave themselves up to the currents of the crowd. The courtyard was reduced to moments – a pair of shoeless feet, a calf struggling against its halter, an hysterical woman – and when the storm passed as abruptly as it had arrived Kostya found himself at the edge of a clearing beneath the cathedral's seven broad steps, his mother's arm tightening round his shoulders.

With the industry of woodcutters, a team of men was slaughtering the animals. Their long hair flew with the turn of their heads. Their linen shirts wore a patina of blood. In a continual stream, the victims were led to a place where the ice had already turned crimson, their rear legs seized and dragged backwards until their front legs splayed, and even in that moment they would look with interest or confusion at the crowd, who were crossing themselves as if subject to a fit, or else reach for some blade of grass protruding from the bloody slush. Sometimes the axe would fail to pass cleanly through an animal's windpipe, and its head would flap wildly from the blood-spouting tatters of its throat. Once the neck was severed both the body and the head would continue to move for a minute or more so that, in one monstrous pile, the decapitated corpses of lambs, sheep and calves appeared to be trying to run away, while in another their goggling, blood-sodden heads champed and thrashed their jaws, and, since it was Kostya's affliction to be able to hear animals, to him they screamed in diabolical chorus.

October 1869

In the gloom of dawn, an autumn wind poured down Kopan-skaya Street, around the lime trees and the sputtering gas lamps, between the banks of the still-dark houses. Kostya and Ignat clung to their caps as they followed the wall around Vladimir-skaya Church. Finding the gate, they joined a muddy path, but it was only when they came to the broken door of the south chapel that they saw the other three boys from their class at the gymnasium, huddled in the blackness in their wadded winter coats.

'Oh, great!' said Tomasz, sarcastically. He put his mouth to Kostya's ear. 'Just what we need! A bloody girl!'

'A girl, am I?' Kostya retorted. 'Well, at least I haven't got breasts!'

'If you . . . If you cause any trouble, I swear to God! We said we'd climb till we can see into the prison yard and that's it. Got it? You follow me, and you do what I say!'

The five of them crept among the chapel's vaulted pillars, through pools of water whose ripples made long grey arches across the floor. They crossed the cavernous nave, where the sticks of jackdaws' nests broke beneath their feet and the wind from the tall, empty windows tossed the cobweb tails of the chandeliers. On one high, lime-streaked wall, Kostya made out a picture of God on His golden throne, indicating to His left and His right. He saw men in their hundreds, naked, beseech-ing, and he was not the only one to hesitate in the torrent of air at the foot of the tower.

The steps spiralled upwards into absolute darkness. Twice, Kostya collided with his cousin. Once, he felt himself being shoved backwards so fiercely that it was only the ragged hand-rail that saved him from falling. With unseen fingers, he felt the streams on the blind, turning wall. He climbed until he had lost count of the steps, and when at last they emerged in the lower bell loft he was astonished by their height, by the strength of the wind, by the blood-coloured sky behind the droplet domes of Trifonov Monastery.

Crowding into the eastern aperture, the boys looked down at the threshing trees of Zasorny ravine, the red-tinged walls of the gymnasium, the sliver of yard just visible behind the shining glass on the walls of the city prison. In the half-light, Kostya could understand little that the others were saying, but he smiled when they smiled, echoed their expressions, stretched like them to try to see more, and when Tomasz turned to scale the few remaining steps that led to the upper loft he followed him at once.

Slowly, the remaining quarters of the little city were beginning to take shape. The treetops took on the colour of the sky. The houses to the west revealed the slopes of their roofs, the shadows of doors and windows, the sparse smoke torn from their chimneys. Peering past heads and shoulders, Kostya searched above the prison walls for any indication of a gallows, but still he could see nothing, and so he pushed through the trembling saplings that sprouted from the rotten floorboards, ducked beneath the mould-tangled bell ropes and squeezed past the westerly bell, on to the ledge, where a series of rusty, wire-thin rungs stretched over the eaves towards the summit of the tower.

Five storeys beneath him, the streetlamps made circles in the mud of Kopanskaya Street.

'Come on!' he called. 'It's sunrise in a minute!'

'Kostya!' Ignat hurried towards him. 'Come on, Kostya, don't be stupid!'

'What do you mean, "stupid"? Do you want to see the hanging or don't you?'

'They don't even climb up there at Easter!'

The other boys were gathering around him, their words becoming discernible with the daylight.

'Kostya, come on! We've got to go!'

'Kostya, someone will see you!'

'Look, you show-off!' Tomasz forced his way around the bell, his fat face livid between his fur hat and collar. 'I warned you! Didn't I warn you?'

'Who's the girl now?' said Kostya, laughing.

'Get in here, and I'll show you who's a girl!'

'Too heavy for it, are you?'

'Look, you bloody cripple!' His cousin was shouting now. 'Everybody hates a show-off, and everybody hates you! The only reason we put up with you is because you're deaf! You haven't got the guts to climb up there, anyway, so why don't you just get back in here before you get all of us into trouble!'

Kostya hardly knew how he came to be standing on top of the tower. A sensation came over him such as he had never experienced in his life. It was like the moment in spring when the ice broke on the river, when the cracks ran long and jagged between the banks and the water that had lain cold and docile beneath the surface all winter came boiling into the waiting air. Suddenly, he was looking down on the whole of Vyatka, the circle of the forest, the fingers of the church towers cut out of the sunrise. He was screaming, kicking the parapet with his soft felt boots until, without a sound, a section as big as himself disappeared. Like a treetop, the tower was swaying in the gale. Staggering, almost falling, he seized the gilded cross and tried to wrench it from its setting, and as the last star stole from the morning sky he raged against the boys in the bell loft, and he raged against this miserable city, and he raged against the Earth itself, which pinned him to its surface, wretched as a worm.

*

When Kostya emerged from the bottom of the tower, he felt no more substantial than his skin. The other boys had long since scattered. Only Ignat walked with him, back through the derelict church, the fragments of plaster, the puddles, the gems of broken glass – outside into a mob of women, children and even a privy councillor in white, mud-spattered trousers. His eyes on the birch leaves drowning in the muddy ground, Kostya felt himself grabbed, pushed and shaken. He looked up only when he heard his mother's voice and saw, with distant interest, a misshapen scar on the wall of the church, a pair of holes in the roof around the tower's first floor, a large piece of masonry jutting from the lank grass of the churchyard.

He put up no resistance as she towed him back up Vladimir-skaya Street, between the squat, bored houses, the barren limes, the children who continued to canter around them. On Preo-brazhenskaya Street, a team of carters was trying to move a heavy wagon through the clinging mud. They were whipping their oxen, heaving at the wheels, but all of them stopped to watch this dancing crowd, the slight, gasping woman who dragged her son through the gate at number 19, between the bedraggled lines of her winter cabbages.

'Well?' Maria Ivanovna turned on Kostya wildly. 'Everybody tells me you climbed the tower and threw bricks off the top. Are you going to deny it?'

Lifting his head from the kitchen floor, Kostya saw lights in his mind and lights in the apartment downstairs. At the table, unmoving, Anna, Fekla, Masha and Yekaterina were watching him over their porridge. He saw his mother stumble to the chamber pot in the corner and kneel on the floorboards, her shoulders shaking. He saw her return, heard her voice, clear as it ever had been, but somehow he noticed only the streak of white on her old grey dress, the tiny down of her moustache, the bunching lines around her eyes, the fine new lines that radiated from her lips.

'Konstantin, what on Earth did you think you were doing? For the love of God! You might have killed someone!'

Kostya looked back at his mother in silence. He felt concerned to see her distressed, but still he felt himself apart from this scene – as if he were watching her across some vast, unbridgeable divide. Looking round the room, he saw his baby brother Stanislaw, crying, propped against the wall beside the stove. He saw Ignat standing miserably just inside the door, his thin arms knotted on his chest. Through the pain in his feet, Kostya felt the warm air rising from the apartment downstairs, and with it came a sensation of calm, even languor, and as his mother began once more to speak he realized how much easier it would be for him simply to close his eyes.

*

It was another four days before Kostya returned from the gymnasium to find almost every door and window in the apartment thrown open – although a Siberian wind tore west across Vyatka and the year's first snow concealed the rust of the roofs and the ruts in the streets. Standing at the top of the stairs, in the doorway of the kitchen, he saw little snow figures dancing inside as they would outside, the windows beating against the shutters, the family photographs shivering on the cold brick wall.

'Mama?' he called. 'Anna?'

To his right, the drawing-room door alone was closed. Kostya tried the handle, but it seemed to have been bolted. He knocked, cupped his ear, but he could hear no voices and feel no movement in the floorboards, and so he went into his bedroom, sat down on the bed, wrapped the counterpane round his shoulders and opened *The History of the Steam Engine* – one of the most interesting-looking books that he had found recently in his father's small library. He turned to the first chapter, which concerned the 'elasticity' and 'expansibility' of steam, but neither of these words meant anything to him and he found himself unable even to concentrate on a diagram of an American locomotive with outside cylinders and an unusually conical funnel.

The whole house seemed to tremble when Eduard Ignatyevich arrived at the bottom of their staircase. He was climbing quickly, two steps at a time, the sensation soon complicated by Anna's lighter patter, and as Kostya arrived back in the kitchen he saw his father reach the drawing-room door in three strides – his face pale and wild between his low black hat and his long grey beard.

'Maria!' he shouted.

He fought with the handle, then took a step backwards and levelled his shoulder at a point above the lock.

Kostya watched in astonishment as his father reappeared, holding by the collar the midwife who had delivered little Stanislaw the previous summer. Never in his life had he seen his father raise a hand against anyone in anger, but when the midwife tried to escape his grip he threw her against the wall beneath the coat hooks with such violence that her scarlet headscarf slipped over her eyes and the contents of her bag exploded across the floor.

With a gesture, Eduard Ignatyevich sent Anna back the way that they had come. He vanished once again into the drawing room, while Kostya remained frozen and the midwife scrabbled across the floorboards, collecting her possessions – a pair of scissors, a bar of soap, a blood-soaked handkerchief, some variety of needle – and hobbled off on to the stairs, her crabbed hands covering her face.

'Father?' called Kostya, uncertainly. 'Father, can I do something to help?'

He stood in silence, then, at last, he picked up a water vase, which was turning circles in a puddle near the table, and restored it to its shelf. He picked up a bundle of herbs and returned it to its hook beside the stove. He closed the front door, the outer windows and the winter windows, collected the broom and swept up the snow. He carried four birch logs from the woodpile to the grate, blew on the embers to rouse the flames and then, treading lightly on his still-painful feet, he went to the drawing-room door, which hung ajar, cupped his ear and peered inside.

Beneath the three large panes and the one small pane of the window, Maria Ivanovna was lying among the leaking horsehair of the green velvet couch. Her hair was loose, black at the ends and silver at the roots. Her face was as white as the roofs and the sky. She was covered by an old grey blanket, which rose falteringly with her chest, and under the blanket the upholstery was stained almost black.

Beside her, Eduard Ignatyevich was kneeling with his back to the door, the soles of his boots solid with snow. His head was hanging forwards so that only a trace of his hair was visible above his heavy, black-clad shoulders. Although the window had been closed, around him the room was in chaos. The one-legged table had fallen over, scattering soil and geranium leaves across the narrow, striped carpet, shattering the pot, while his work of philosophy had been carried from the desk to the floor, where its pages described the spiralling path of the wind.

Had Kostya not known his father he might have thought that he was praying.

*

On the table in the icon corner, Maria Ivanovna wore her old black dress with the white lace collar. Two copper coins concealed her eyes. On her chest, she held a cross with a long silver chain, which, as the priest lowered the lid of the coffin, escaped suddenly from her fingers and spilled down her chest in a quick, soft rush. In another life, Kostya might have thrown himself forwards, grasped her hands and found them to be warm, but in this one he remained in line against the blank kitchen wall, beneath the shrouded mirror, in his least-darned trousers and his best linen shirt, and his eyes were hot and his vision indistinct as the priest laid out the pall – as if putting an infant to bed.

He followed his father, his uncle and the two other bearers out of the apartment, down the stairs, into Preobrazhenskaya Street. Through the raging snow, he saw the man from number 22, who was beating his wife with the buckle of his belt – although he stopped when he saw the funeral procession, and the two of them rose, removed their hats and crossed themselves with three fingers. At the Assembly of Nobles, a handful of revellers was emerging from a night-long ball – garrison officers in tight white trousers, ladies in silk now that crinoline had fallen out of favour, their bosoms bare to the aching cold – and since the Tsiolkovsky family were nobles themselves they acknowledged the coffin with a dip of their heads before they climbed into a fur-lined troika.

Beyond the priest, his lilac cope and grubby sledge, Kostya made out *izvozchiki* turning down side streets as if realizing suddenly that they were going the wrong way. On Preobrazhenskaya Street, they met no vehicles or pedestrians at all, and when the procession steered north on to Vladimirskaya Street so they turned into the wind and even the alternating skeletons of the lime trees and the gas lamps vanished into the blizzard.

Kostya imagined that he had left the curving surface of the Earth, that he was climbing past the tower of Vladimirskaya Church, through the thick clouds, into those exalted regions where the geese would pass in an arrow in the spring and the autumn and Vyatka would be no more than a speck in the illimitable forest – barely seen and instantly forgotten. He imagined himself emerging, as if through a gateway, into the glistening ether, where he would step on to a small, passing planet that he would name Konstantin after himself and he would drive as easily as a team of horses. Konstantin would be a place of no change, its leaves and flowers perennially in early summer. As tsar, Kostya would abolish death and allow no limit either to food or transport. He would build a railway in a belt around the equator, where a 4-2-4 would travel at a perpetual 123 versts per hour, its smoke rising in a spiral into space, and as he ate meat pies on the velvet cushions of his private carriage he would lean from his window to regard the passing stars, to lift his hat to Mercury and Mars.

Konstantin

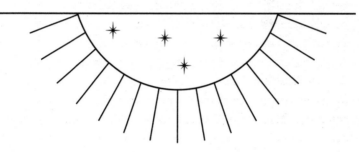

January 1873

'The very large numbers, which are so often met with in Astronomy,' wrote Amédée Guillemin in *The Heavens*, 'leave for the most part only a very vague impression on the mind. It is difficult for the imagination to figure the objects that they represent; and where it is a question even of moderate distances, it is only by the aid of comparisons that we can arrive at any precise idea. If these distances are greater than those which we can actually see on a terrestrial horizon, say than 40 or 70 versts, the image properly so called vanishes, and we are compelled to have recourse to other means of representation; for example, we ask how much time a locomotive, going at a known rate, will require to traverse the given distance. The idea of duration comes then in aid of space to complete and perfect it.

'Let us see with what exactness we can by this means form a conception of the distance which separates the Earth from the Sun.

'Light – the propagation of which is the most rapid movement known, and which travels at the rate of 290,000 versts in a second of time – requires 8 minutes and 17 seconds to flash from the Sun to the Earth. If we suppose the intervening space to contain atmospheric air, a sound, with an intensity sufficiently great to put in motion a sphere of such enormous dimensions, would take fourteen years and two months to reach our ears, sound travelling, as we know, about 340 metres a second.

'Finally, an express train going at the rate of about 50 versts an hour, leaving the Earth the 1st of January, 1866, would not arrive at the Sun until the year 2213, nearly 347 years after the day of its departure.

'We can thus form an idea of the immensity of the chasm which lies between the Sun and our globe – an immensity, the measure of which is expressed by the round number, so simple in appearance, of 140 million versts. It is this number – this 140 million versts – which will henceforth form the unit, the "standard measure", by means of which the other celestial distances will be expressed.'

*

Konstantin counted the seven zeroes, then counted them again. He considered how much further it was to the Sun than Vladivostok, and with a little rounding down and a sum on the back of his Latin grammar he came to the figure 23,333⅓, which still possessed almost no meaning for him at all. He twisted the scraps of moustache that sprouted at each end of his mouth, pulled his sheepskin tightly round his shoulders and turned to the open window of the classroom and the Sun itself, which burnt above the snow-shrouded roof of the prison and threw its light from every plane and contour of the embankments and the snow-bowed trees in Zasorny ravine. He looked askance, through the haze of the city's smoke, and, by narrowing his eyes, he managed to see an orange disc about the same size as the Moon. He tried to imagine how big and fierce the Sun would appear if he were standing directly in front of it, but the exercise proved impossible, and so in the end he contented himself with the view from Mercury.

Finding the relevant page in *The Heavens*, he discovered that at 44,200,000 versts, the nearest point in Mercury's orbit, the Sun would be 3¼ times larger than it appeared from the Earth: a furnace consuming the sky, its heat increased by 6⅔.

Although the day was calm, the smoke rising at a gentle angle from the chimneys across the ravine, still Konstantin failed to hear the bell that marked the end of the lesson. He knew it had rung only by the stirring of the other twenty-four boys, whose backs straightened, whose pencils vanished, whose arms returned to the sleeves of their coats. On the bench beside him, Ignat made a tapering pile of his books. In his place by the stove, Tomasz consulted the watch in the pocket of his thick woollen waistcoat. At the front of the room, the Latin master continued to pass back and forth beneath the meaningless characters on the blackboard, his voice a sequence of half-heard grunts, his step the same short-legged strut that had measured out the past hour, but already Konstantin could feel the next-door class disgorging on to the floorboards in the corridor – their footsteps evaporating as they reached the top of the long stone staircase.

Out on Kopanskaya Street, Konstantin left the crowds at the gymnasium gates – laughing, pushing one another, no doubt sending jibes in his direction. He hurried alone along the icy pavement, the Sun warm like candlelight on his downy left cheek, his nose grown distinctly sharp, his eyelids showing a tendency to droop. Turning on to Tsarevskaya Street, he paced out the distance between the streetlamps. He wondered how Amédée Guillemin could possibly know that it was 140 million versts from the Earth to the Sun, and as he passed beneath the fire wardens smoking in the bell tower of Tsarevo-Konstantinovskaya Church he tried to imagine some way to measure the size and distance of the Moon, and then to scale up these measurements, but by the time he reached Preobrazhenskaya Street he had rejected this idea, and he frowned to himself as he climbed the stairs to the apartment.

In the kitchen, Anna was preparing cabbage soup – one eye on little Stanislaw, who was scurrying after a spring-powered carriage.

'One hundred and forty million versts away!' Konstantin exclaimed.

'What is?' she asked.

'The Sun!'

The problem with so much of Konstantin's reading was the endless words that he did not understand. The language of mathematics seemed to come to him naturally – even cube roots and cosines needed minimal explanation – but as he sat at his father's desk in the drawing room, opened *The Heavens* and turned to a chapter named 'Celestial Measurements', on the very first page he encountered the words 'inaccessible', 'stellar', 'parallax', 'unacquainted', 'enunciating' and 'incredulity'. He might have abandoned the book altogether had he not spotted, on the following page, a picture of a man in a field beside a river, measuring the distance to the top of a church tower with a mysterious, three-legged instrument.

Konstantin considered this instrument, a theodolite, with interest. He rummaged through *The Heavens* but, finding no further information on the subject, he turned to the shelves that held his father's dust-covered manuscript and various books on science, mathematics and natural history. On page 4 of Adolphe Ganot's *Elementary Treatise on Physics*, he discovered that a theodolite measured angles, but it was only in a book named *Practical Geodesy* that he found a description of sufficient detail to start work.

He took his father's protractor from the desk drawer and, with a piece of sealing wax, attached a length of string to the meeting point of the radial lines. He tied a kopeck coin to the end of the string and opened the window. As he understood it, the principle of the theodolite was to make a geometric shape in actual space just as you would draw one on paper. If he called the windowsill A, the pavement directly beneath the window B, and the foot of the tower of Tsarevo-Konstantinovskaya Church C, then he had a right-angled triangle with one side that he could measure easily with the tape that his father used on the logs at the sawmill. Breathing uncomfortably, Konstantin lay on his belly so that his head poked outside into the sunlight. He unrolled the tape until its end touched the ground and measured 4.81 arshins to the corner of the frame. He realized at once, however, that it was impossible to use the theodolite at that level, and so he measured an additional 0.19 arshins to make five, crouched down, checked the level again, propped his elbows inside the window in the manner of a tripod, peered along the flat edge of the protractor until it was aligned with the point where the tower met the crumpled snow, and clamped off the string against the notches of the angles.

Konstantin closed the window and took down the tangent tables from their shelf. If the angle A was 89.3°, he concluded, then the angle C was 0.7°, the angles of a triangle making 180°. He ran a finger down the columns of tiny printed figures and wrote in chalk on his slate:

$$\text{Tan } 0.7° = 0.012218$$
$$\therefore 0.012218 = 5 \div \text{distance to tower}$$
$$\therefore 5 \div 0.012218 = \text{distance to tower}$$

He pondered a moment, then divided 50,000 by 122 and wrote on the slate:

$$409.8 \text{ arshins.}$$

Standing on the pavement some minutes later, when only the dormer windows of 19 Preobrazhenskaya Street still reflected the afternoon sunlight, Konstantin tied his ankles together with string so that his feet were precisely one arshin apart. He set one heel against the pink brick wall beneath the neighbours' kitchen window, waited for a government clerk to pass on a pair of skis, took a sight along his left arm and set out into the Thursday traffic.

He progressed slowly, keeping one foot exactly in front of the other, glancing back from time to time to check his path in the snow. Dimly, he was conscious of the noises around him. He knew that the peasants were stopping to watch him, laughing, mimicking his walk in their spotless market-day shoes and stockings, but his experiment exercised all of his attention and even when the girl from number 23 appeared at her front door in a blue velvet cloak, Arctic in her beauty, he was able to absorb her in a universal mosaic of circles, rhombi, trapezoids and triangles.

March 1873

'The *ear trumpet*,' wrote Adolphe Ganot in *Elementary Treatise on Physics*, 'is used by persons who are hard of hearing. It is essentially an inverted speaking trumpet, and consists of a conical metallic tube, one of whose extremities, terminating in a *bell*, receives the sound, while the other end is introduced into the ear. This instrument is the reverse of the speaking trumpet. The bell serves as mouthpiece; that is, it receives the sounds coming from the mouth of the person who speaks. These sounds are transmitted by a series of reflections to the interior of the trumpet, so that the waves, which would become greatly developed, are concentrated on the auditory apparatus, and produce a far greater effect than divergent waves would have done.'

April 1873

Even by his own standards, Eduard Ignatyevich looked grim and preoccupied. In the three and a half years since the death of his wife, he seemed to have weathered like an exposed pine, bent by the wind and bowed by the snow so that even during the fine, brief summers he was unable to recover his previous shape. In the late-spring sunlight flooding through the south-facing window of the drawing room, he stood grey-faced, red-eyed, considering through the perpetual miasma of his cigarette smoke a letter written in a formal hand.

Hesitantly, Konstantin rose from the desk, directed his ear trumpet towards his father's lips.

'What is that, Konstantin?'

His voice was so plain that he might have been speaking directly into his ear.

'It's . . . It's an ear trumpet, Father.'

'An "ear trumpet",' he repeated, tonelessly.

'Yes, Father . . .'

'Yes.' Eduard Ignatyevich took a step forwards. His eyes turned momentarily to the long tin shaft, the funnel bell, the knotted bands of wire taken from the heaps of crinoline that Konstantin had bought for kopecks at the flea market. 'Well, Konstantin, it will come as no surprise to you to learn that you have failed the second year for a second time, which means, of course, that you will receive no qualification. I am afraid that I can see no alternative to an apprenticeship.' He removed his spectacles, rubbed his eyes with hard, blunt fingers. 'Given the sacrifices I have made to pay your fees at the gymnasium, I need hardly tell you how disappointed I am in you. If you had dedicated a fraction of the energy to your schoolwork that you have wasted on these toys of yours . . .' He indicated a carriage of wood and tin, which sat on the grubby grey blanket covering the green velvet couch.

Konstantin lowered his eyes, opened his mouth.

'Do you have something to say for yourself?'

'They're . . . They're not toys, Father. They're models.'

'I hardly see that it makes any difference.'

'But . . . models are essential to an understanding of physics, that's what Adolphe Ganot says.'

'Indeed?' Eduard Ignatyevich collected the carriage, revolved it in his hands. 'So, tell me, what physical principle does this little car demonstrate that is more important than your school certificate?'

'It's a reaction machine, Father . . . It's propelled by a jet of steam, so it . . . it demonstrates the Third Law of Isaac Newton.'

His father looked again at the neat wooden wheels, the firebox, the slim tubulure that jutted from the back of the cylindrical boiler.

'Explain,' he said, after a moment.

'Well, Father,' said Konstantin, haltingly. 'It moves because of the reactive force of the vapour expelled by the boiling water, which proves . . . that for every action there is an equal and opposite reaction.'

Eduard Ignatyevich extinguished his cigarette in the fireplace. Through the clearing smoke, the sunlight found a trace of blue in his eyes.

'Then . . . how do you explain the others?'

'Well, Father . . .' Konstantin turned to the jumble of models in the corner. 'I've . . . I've made a carriage driven by a spring, which . . . demonstrates the principle of potential energy, and a theodolite, which makes extremely accurate angular measurements, and I've built a lathe, and a pendulum clock, and . . . I've tried to make a hydrogen balloon to demonstrate the buoyancy of a gas less dense than air, but unfortunately I have no caou . . . no caoutchouc varnish so I have not yet been able to stop the gas from escaping. And I've made lots of inventions too! I've made a new type of string instrument with a bow you can work with a pedal! And I've made a new type of carriage powered by a windmill, with a special tail so that the sails will always face into the wind!'

*

Sitting in the stern of one of the broad, shallow boats at the wharf beneath the big hotel, Konstantin watched as the ferryman seized his oars and began to pull with quick, fierce strokes – angling his course into the current. He felt a shudder in the hull as the first ice-trimmed log collided with the gunwale. In the prow, he saw the three women returning from the Sunday market with their unsold figurines and penny whistles cross themselves, lower their heads, and so, to provide a distraction, he rolled his reaction machine first one way then the other across the lid of a brightly painted chest. When he looked up, he saw that he had attracted the attention of the women and the ferryman alike, but such was the roar of the wind and the river in his ear trumpet that he was unable to hear any trace of their questions. He watched as his father explained the principle of reaction, while, above his old black hat, the spires of Feodorovskaya Church, Pyatnitsky Church, Spassky Cathedral and Holy Resurrection Cathedral emerged from the glimmering, snow-strewn escarpment – as if ascending into the heavens.

On the narrow beach at Dymkovo, Konstantin and Eduard Ignatyevich walked among keeling boats, men casting lines and boys scavenging for planks in the ocean of logs that spread upstream from the boom at Simonovsky Island. They passed teams of horses dragging logs up the bank on long, looped ropes – following the principle of the pulley. They passed gangs of peasants loading firewood on to sledges whose runners made streams in the ruined ground. They passed bonfires tall as two-storey houses, a pair of rails where men pushed logs on wagons towards the hulking shed of the sawmill itself – its tall black chimney boiling smoke, its circular saw screaming so plainly that, for a moment, Konstantin almost thought that his hearing had returned.

Overlooking this infernal activity, a bare-cheeked, yellow-haired figure was smoking on the veranda of a small, grimy office. He was dressed in polished leather boots and a suit in the German fashion – a golden ribbon between his lapels – and he lifted his hat when he saw them approaching between the stacks of boards and beams, bowing ceremonially.

'Eduard!' he exclaimed. 'And what do we have here? A bugler?'

Konstantin glanced questioningly at his father.

'Matvei Ilyich,' said Eduard Ignatyevich. 'May I present my son, Konstantin? I am afraid that he is rather hard of hearing. He is employing an ear trumpet of his own invention.'

'Of his own invention!' The foreman raised an eyebrow. 'A boy after my own heart! And tell me, young man, what is that extraordinary-looking carriage you have there?'

'It's . . . a reaction machine, sir,' said Konstantin.

'Is it indeed?'

'Yes, sir . . .'

'The Third Law of Isaac Newton, eh?'

'Yes, sir . . .'

'I should say so!' Matvei Ilyich chuckled amiably. 'I hope you will honour me with a demonstration?'

So thick were the soot and the sawdust on the windows of the office that, despite the bright spring sunshine, a lantern was burning on the leather-clad desk, which was largely concealed by an enormous technical diagram. The light caught the spines of the fat, dusty ledgers in the bookcase. It shone from a portrait of Alexander II and a recent, framed cutting from the St Petersburg *Vedomosti*.

'Tell me, Matvei Ilyich,' said Eduard Ignatyevich when they were all sitting down. 'How was your reception with the governor?'

'It was, I believe, a success . . .' The foreman produced a silver cigarette case. 'Of course, Mikhail Yakovlevich is not a scientific man like ourselves, but he is a politician and a reader of the newspapers. He has given me his assurance that he will speak to Prince Kuznetsov on our behalf.'

Konstantin held a match to the crumpled paper in the firebox of the reaction machine and blew on the woodchips until they were burning fiercely. He set the model on the floorboards, and turned his attention to the diagram on the desk. It took him several moments to identify a pair of giant wheels at the heart of its labyrinth of struts, levers, ropes and regulatory instruments – vertically arranged, strung with a belt of neat little barrels. So far as he could tell, the right-hand side of this belt was immersed in a tall thin reservoir of water, while a drive shaft led from the lower of the two wheels, passed through a system of gears and concluded in a minute circle, which was, he realized, the blade of the sawmill itself.

Konstantin frowned and restored the ear trumpet.

'And since it seems a certainty, Matvei Ilyich,' his father was saying, his cigarette pinched between his fingers, 'that your machine will need to be replicated throughout the country, even throughout the world, it occurred to me that . . . that perhaps the time has come for you to consider employing an . . . apprentice. As you see, my son shows considerable technical potential.'

The foreman nodded, joined his hands beneath his naked chin.

'Sir?' asked Konstantin, cautiously. 'May I ask you a question?'

'By all means, my boy!'

'Sir, I . . . I am not sure that I fully understand this diagram. It seems to me that the machine is propelled by the barrels rising through the tank of water, and if this is the case then it should continue . . .'

'Perpetually,' said his father, with satisfaction.

'Perpetually,' Konstantin repeated. He looked again at the diagram. 'But, sir, I am afraid that I do not yet understand the principle. You see . . . My understanding is that the buoyancy of an object, either in air or water, is the result of the difference in pressure between its upper and lower surfaces? That is to say, if you have an empty barrel immersed in water then the pressure on the lower surface will be greater than the pressure on the upper surface, which causes an overall upward force . . .'

Matvei Ilyich nodded his assent.

'But . . . But, sir, surely if a series of barrels are connected to one another, and they stretch both in and out of the water, then effectively they become a single object. And, if that is the case, then surely there is no difference in pressure between the upper and lower surfaces?'

'What are you trying to say?' asked the foreman, his smile beginning to fracture.

'Well, sir . . . If there is no difference in pressure then surely the machine would not move?'

The reaction machine was coming to the boil. As the first

steam spewed from the tubulure, it began to lumber across the floorboards.

'Konstantin,' said his father, in a low, icy voice. 'Matvei Ilyich is a member of the Russian Physico-Chemical Society. His machine has not only been approved by his peers, it has been acclaimed by the press in the capital itself.' He indicated the newspaper cutting on the wall. 'I believe that you owe him an apology.'

'Well, Father, I do not wish to cause any offence . . .'

'An apology, if you please.'

'But, Father –'

'Konstantin! Stop this!'

Reaching the bookcase, the reaction machine wobbled, turned, met the adjacent wall at a shallower angle and resumed its journey back towards the desk – its jet of steam growing in length and force, the lantern reflected in its cylindrical boiler.

Wincing, Eduard Ignatyevich pushed himself to his feet, and so Konstantin did the same. The two of them faced one another in the dingy light, and suddenly Konstantin realized that he was taller than his father. Behind the cloud of his cigarette smoke and the cloud-like scratches on the lenses of his spectacles, Eduard Ignatyevich fought to stand upright. He stared at his son with open fury, but his eyes were small between their heavy lids and the long white beard on his wizened cheeks, and his shoulders remained the stooping, suffering shoulders of an old man.

June 1873

And so he saw the tall grass in the endless fields, moving in chorus with the evening breeze. He saw the haymakers who followed the contours, swinging their scythes in martial rhythm. He saw the sky-blue notes of the cornflowers, the dandelions clamouring on the banks. He saw the light that rang from the surface of the river – beneath the three tight folds of his belly, his naked feet, the prow of the sleepily revolving praam. As the shadows extended from the willows and the birches, he felt a tiny, stinging sensation on his back, and he turned to find the captain, Vasily Vasilyevich, sitting astride the pitched plank roof, his brightly coloured Circassian overcoat spilling around his bare brown chest. Removing the stem of his tobacco pipe from his lips, Vasily Vasilyevich grinned at the precision of his aim. He leant backwards to mime a fanfare, and so Konstantin rose and handed him his ear trumpet – which he used to play a three-note summons to dinner.

Konstantin crossed the bales of linen – claret, mauve and indigo, still faintly acrid from the dye-works – and descended the ladder into the cabin at the stern. Already the crew were sitting in a circle around the big wooden bowl: a dozen wiry, sunburnt figures, travelling to the Volga to work as fishermen, barge haulers or stokers on the steamboats. Like them, he removed his cap, washed his hands and crossed himself ten times. He took his bread and salt, and waited for the captain's daughter, Katya, to pour the soup from the iron pot that hung from the beam above the little fire. He ate, and, since even with his ear trumpet he could never hear anything when he was eating, he studied each of the men in turn, following their laughter, their wild gesticulations suggestive of an enormous fish or fluvial monster. That way, he was able to look briefly, without embarrassment, at Katya: a small, neat girl of about fifteen, one eye asquint beneath her long, dark lashes, her single plait escaping from a bright green headscarf, a gap showing between her front teeth when she smiled.

*

The best thing about these long, light evenings was that Konstantin could read until eleven or even later without so much as tiring his eyes. On his perch on the prow, he looked once more through *The Heavens*, which he had found in his bag with his blanket, his passport, his sheepskin, his spare socks from Anna and his letter of introduction to a man named Professor Brachmann at the Imperial Technical School in Moscow. He read that Sirius possessed a diameter of 17 million versts, twelve times greater than the Sun. He read that, excepting the Sun, the nearest star was Alpha Centauri, at the 'fearful distance' of 29 trillion versts, and that the naked eye could perceive, at most, about five thousand stars, but that with the twenty-fut reflector telescope built in England by Sir William Herschel it was possible to see more than 20 million. Already Konstantin knew most of these figures by heart, but still he liked to read them over again, and then, as if digesting, to watch some scene on the ever-changing river. In this way, he saw nightjars wrinkling the water. He saw columns of mosquitoes among the willows and the alders. He saw boys splashing beneath clusters of diagonally patterned houses, and peasants paddling from their villages to the hay fields, where, despite fourteen hours of mowing, raking and binding, they sang and danced against the fire-coloured sky.

When, at last, some impression of darkness fell over the

Vyatka, Konstantin scaled the roof where Vasily Vasilyevich continued his vigil, and he lay down on the ridgepole, his head towards the prow, his arms and his legs spilling to either side of him, watching the stars turn as slowly as the praam. To the south, he saw Orion, his belt protruding from the dark, shining river, and as he followed its line he came to Aldebaran, the eye of the Bull, and since he had nothing else whatsoever to do he narrowed his eyes to bring it into focus and simply watched its scintillations: a sequence of colours more rapid than he could begin to apprehend, their root note red, like lust or fury.

'Aldebaran . . .' he breathed.

He felt a hand on his shoulder and reached for his ear trumpet.

'What did you say?' asked the captain.

'Aldebaran!' Konstantin repeated, in the same, marvelling voice.

'What's that?'

'It's a red star of the first magnitude.' He had still not moved his eyes. 'It lies at a distance of sixty-eight light years from the Earth, which is to say . . . about 700 trillion versts. If you were to travel there by express train it would take . . . something in the region of 22 million years.'

Vasily Vasilyevich laughed a low, friendly laugh, his breath hot with spirit. 'You talk just like a book, you do,' he said. 'Anyone ever tell you that?'

Konstantin was almost asleep when he felt a tremor in the boards and the long, heavy stirring of the great boat ceased. He opened his eyes to see Vasily Vasilyevich already on his feet, calling to somebody in the darkness, beckoning to him urgently before he vanished off the end of the roof.

On the deck, most of the bargemen were already scrambling on to the ladder, into the shallow water where the current was visible in the stars, in the launch hanging downstream at the length of its rope, in the filament shadows of the fishing lines. Konstantin removed his shirt and his ear trumpet and lowered himself past the massive hull until he felt the fine sand between his toes. Around him, he saw identical skies between dark, symmetrical banks. The bargemen were black beneath the looming barge, charting the sandbank, and soon they congregated near the prow where the water came barely to their knees, turned to one another, pointed and shook their heads so that their shaggy hair snaked across their shoulders.

Konstantin set his hands to the great, corrugated wall, gripped the iron rivets between his fingers, closed his eyes, smelt the meat-like oakum in the cracks, the engrained stench of the men pressed around him. He felt the minnows nibbling at the hairs of his ankles. He pushed until there were colours in his eyelids, and when he looked again he realized that Katya had arrived in the space beside him, her smell exquisite, alien as the water, and so he pushed until he was shouting with the effort, and when at last the stern caught the current so the Vyatka became itself once more and he fell forwards, his head emerging from the heavens like a god's.

*

At the confluence of the Kama and the Volga, the steamboats crawled across the iron-grey water, trailing smoke as black as the clouds and pairs of waves on which fishermen rolled and tossed. Sitting on the roof, Vasily Vasilyevich raised flags of greeting and negotiation to willow-lashed rafts and other barges heavy with rye and barley, soap and glass, potash and gun carriages, and in time a steamboat with a bright red funnel appeared alongside them – a man in a fluttering coat lifting his low, peaked cap among the piles of birch logs. He called to the helmsman and as the twin wheels span and the tug approached the prow a deckhand threw a well-coiled rope across the intervening foam – attached to a second rope as thick as his leg.

The rope rose, snapped tight, jerked the praam forwards, fell, slapped the water.

'I tell you, boy,' said Vasily Vasilyevich, appearing beneath the roof. The first fat raindrops exploded on the open deck. 'I tell you, you young ones don't know how easy you've got it. Back when I was a boy, well, that was thirty years ago now. These days there's five hundred steamers on the Volga, give or take, but back then you could count them on your hands . . . See them woods?' He gestured past the churning paddle wheels at a wilderness of tree stumps and limestone cliffs. 'It wasn't just the hauling, which was no kind of fun, I can tell you. Still isn't, I shouldn't wonder. Back then, the woods come right down to the water, and the woods, they was chock-full of bandits! Chock-full! You never knew when they was going to come leaping out on you!'

Among the tangled clouds, there was a perceptible shimmering, and the captain counted out versts on his fingers.

'You see, I was working for Demidov in them days. The iron foundry, north of Nizhny Tagil? Well, you know how they get the iron out of there? Old Demidov, he put up the biggest dams you ever saw. Lakes thirty versts end to end! Ten from side to side! As God's my witness . . . All through the winter we was building him praams on the riverbed, filling them with pipes, sheets, nails, spades, trays, anything you could make out of iron, and then, come the thaw, we'd say our prayers and, bam! Up come the floodgates! Two hundred versts on a wave we'd go! Over rapids! Round bends like horseshoes! That's the thin end of the wedge, that is. There weren't a trick we didn't learn . . .'

Again, the bleeding roof shone white.

'Because if we got stuck, that was it, you see? If you met a bank or a rock, you'd got to get off him that bloody moment or that praam weren't going nowhere till next year. You see, you need to know the tricks if you're going to get to Nizhny. You can't beat experience. And on the Volga, well, if you don't know the steamboat captains they'll hold you to ransom. If you don't pay they'll leave you to the mercies of Old Man Caspian!' He smiled amicably, fine lines fanning from his eyes. 'Be sure and mention that to your uncle, won't you? If you should happen to be writing . . .'

*

Two days later, Konstantin looked past the Tatars making their afternoon obeisances on the paddle-boxes of the tugboat at the whitewashed towers of Nizhny Novgorod, at a chaos of masts, rafts, ornate barges and ones as plain as their own, of two-storey passenger ships where ladies with parasols shielded their pale skin from the feverish Sun, and steamboats in such numbers that the skein of their smoke seemed to truss up the sky. As the crew tied up on the Siberian Wharf, which stretched three versts along the north bank of the Makaryev Fair, a ragged army of labourers descended on the praam, shouting for work, showing their strength by tearing planks from the roof. The captain sprang on to the dock in a pink cravat and a waistcoat with bright copper buttons, while Konstantin spent unnecessary minutes pulling on his boots, checking the contents of his bag, tucking his hair beneath his cap.

'Vasily Vasilyevich?' he asked finally, as he scaled the rope ladder. He looked warily at the teeming traffic. 'Vasily Vasilyevich? Could you direct me to the station, please?'

'Lord, you are in a hurry!' The captain laughed, turned to the labourers, glanced at the dust-smothered Sun. 'Well, this lot reckon you might have about forty minutes. You might just about make it, but we've still got the better part of a roof over our heads. There'll be another train first thing in the morning. Why not wait the night?'

'I . . . I think I ought to get to Moscow.'

The captain nodded and put a friendly arm round his shoulder. He peered across the linen bales towards the cabin at the stern, where his daughter was cleaning the pots. She smiled, curtsied, appeared to look at both of them at once.

Konstantin followed Katya among carts laden with grain and watermelons, past mountains of cotton in which their own cargo would have been swallowed in a moment, and empty praams where men were working with saws and axes. On the end of the peninsula, the half-built cathedral had acquired red paint and black roofs in the five years that he had been away. Sometimes the two of them walked side by side and Konstantin inspected a slender island, which had appeared in the Oka – bristling with barges, piled with iron in every imaginable form. Sometimes Katya led the way and he watched the lilt of her hips beneath her long green skirt, the dance of her neat leather boots, the long dark plait whose tip flicked like a tail beneath her silver belt.

Together they wormed their way among men with brown skin and black beards, along a boulevard of bearskins, fox skins, wolfskins, bundles of paper, stinking sterlet, grindstones, wine-skins, skittering rats and seething flies.

'Sir?' called Katya, as they arrived in a square of shops with pointed roofs and curious, molten corners. Her voice was shrill, with the easy confidence of her father. 'If you don't mind me asking, how are you going to be a student if you can't hear properly? I mean, students have teachers and lessons and things, don't they? Like in a school?'

'Well . . . Well, Yekaterina Vasilyevna,' said Konstantin, hesitantly. Their eyes met momentarily round the bell of his ear trumpet. 'I have a letter for a professor who used to teach my father at the Forestry Institute in Petersburg. I hope that he might help me. Or else, I believe that there is a free library in Moscow. I might be able to go there . . .'

'You never been to Moscow before, then?'

Konstantin shook his head. 'I've never even been on a train. Well . . . When I was a boy we used to live in Ryazan and sometimes we used to run and hang on the back, but that's all. It doesn't really count . . .'

Katya laughed, glanced towards a crescent-crowned mosque, which loomed out of the dust cloud. He guessed that she had heard the fifteen-minute whistle.

'You're brave, you are,' she said, simply.

Crossing a bridge above a canal apparently used to drain the latrines, they left the cobbles and joined the tides of merchants in a swamp-like street, fighting their way among ox-carts, itinerant vendors of tea and rabbit skins, beggars with suppurating sores. Plainly, the fair spread for many versts beyond its central shops. They passed two men fighting in a circle, an enclosure of plunging horses, a tireless succession of stalls selling rags, jugs of kerosene, boxes of tea, and Konstantin was just beginning to hope that he would miss the train, after all, when they emerged in the courtyard of a large white mansion.

On the muddy wooden platform, the five-minute whistle seemed already to have gone. There were mobs around the steps to the third-class carriages. Women were weeping and waving pocket handkerchiefs. Even the four cavalry officers Konstantin noticed through a first-class window appeared to be throwing down their cards with particular animation. Beneath a two-headed eagle at the mouth of the station, the locomotive, its two leading wheels, four driving wheels and conical funnel, were almost invisible for the steam erupting from its long, black pistons.

Suddenly, Katya stretched, closed her eyes and kissed him with soft, strong lips. He heard the clack of her teeth against his own. He tasted the tang of her saliva, felt the pressure of her small, neat nose, but by the time he realized what was happening the train was moving and she was dancing back into the anonymity of the fair.

July 1873

The following morning, the July sunlight bore down on Moscow. It threw heat from the cobbles, from bleached stone walls whose every crack and blemish it exposed, from green iron roofs that must hardly have cooled down during the night. Outside Yaroslavsky Station, Konstantin emerged from the hordes of *izvozchiki*, who ignored him to a man, and arrived on a broad street empty except for a two-storey tramcar, blinds on the sunny side, moving as ponderously as its white-hooded horses. He went to sit on the scalded grass in the shade of a birch tree, untied his bag and took out *The Heavens*, a hunk of black bread, a bottle of water, his sheepskin, his blanket, his socks and his passport.

The letter was gone.

Konstantin turned the bag upside down. He shook the blanket, leafed through the book, rifled in the pockets of his coat, even checked the purse in his waistband. Dazed with sleeplessness, he looked at the people in the square beneath the tall white station, and at this distance, like some terrible joke, every one of them seemed to be somebody he knew. A stiff little man was the Latin master, Alexei Ilyich Rednikov. A spherical gentleman in a calèche was Stanislaw Ignatyevich. A young woman in a bonnet was his sister Anna.

He must have fallen asleep in the end, since he discovered suddenly that he was sitting in the brutal sunlight, and that a string of carts was hauling iron out of the square, their cargo shimmering, their wheels thunderous even to him. He looked over his shoulder at the clock on the turret of Ryazansky Station, which told him it was early afternoon. He took out his bottle, drank several mouthfuls, splashed some water on his burning face. He remembered his letter and pored once again through his bag and his pockets. He stared at a pond where fishermen lay among the trees, watching their floats through half-closed eyes, then, since he could think of no other course of action, he decided to follow the directions that he had been given by the ticket inspector. He got to his feet and turned south on to Krasnoselsky Street – crossing the tracks of which he had dreamt a thousand times, which followed the telegraph wires back through Kolomna, Voskresensk and Lyubertsy, all the way home to Ryazan.

Moscow was nothing like Konstantin had imagined. Unlike the neat grid of Vyatka, its streets seemed to meander wildly in any direction they chose: dusty and unpaved, as if the city were not the consummation of civilization, after all, but merely a gargantuan village. He passed triangle-topped mansions and monumental churches, but more often than not he walked through a riot of little wooden houses, red, green, white and yellow, windmills with sleeping sails, yards where a cow or two stood tethered in a circle of dry, shorn grass or a group of peasants was drinking in the shade.

For perhaps half an hour, he stood beneath a lime tree on Nemetskaya Street, gazing across an arching drive and hemispherical garden at the tawny palace of the Imperial Moscow Technical School – imagining in every window libraries, lecture theatres, laboratories equipped with every air pump, compound microscope and voltaic pile available to technology. He watched young men in bow ties come bounding down the steps into the sunlight, recoil comically and tip their caps over their eyes. He watched them climb into droshkies, or retire beneath the dense, strange trees – words darting between them like light. Several times he steeled himself to enter the gates, to find the professor and explain to him that he would like to become one of his students – although he had no letter, and he would be unable to hear his lectures, and his ragged clothes were stained with rust, dust, sweat and dye.

*

It was late afternoon when Konstantin decided that he would have to find somewhere to wash and sleep before he made any attempt to enter the university, and so, his empty water bottle dangling from his hand, he returned slowly back up Nemetskaya Street, keeping to the shadows on the left-hand side, peering through eyes struggling to focus at the notices of rooms to let. He found one pink house covered in plaster impressions of naked children where an attic was available for twenty roubles a month. He found rooms or sleeping places in several of the wooden houses for six roubles, even five, and once he summoned up the confidence to knock and attempt to negotiate, but by the time he reached a small Old Believers' Church at a bend in the road and saw ahead of him the junction with Olkhovskaya Street he was so thirsty and exhausted that he was ready to collapse in the churchyard.

Across the street, a washerwoman was hoisting a rope from a well, her spotted dress spotted further with dust, soap and water, her lips turned down with the effort. As she set the earthenware pot on the ground, the muscles showed long and hard in her thin, bare arms. She waited while her daughter – a skinny creature with one leg shorter than the other – tied its handle to a yoke, then she paused to cough, her face pale and drawn in the tiring sunlight.

'Excuse me, madam?' Konstantin approached the pair cautiously. 'I am sorry to intrude, but might you be able to spare me a drink of water, please?'

The washerwoman looked up, crossed herself sharply.

'It . . . It's not . . .' he stammered. 'It's not . . . It just helps me to hear, madam. I would just like some water, if I may?'

She looked at him again, then nodded guardedly and watched as he filled up his bottle and drank in gulps, which turned instantly to sweat on his dust-covered face.

'Thank you, madam,' he said.

'What's all this "madam" business? You ain't blind as well, are you?'

'No, madam.'

'Just come off the train, I suppose?'

'Yes . . .'

The washerwoman sighed, and her face slackened. She had grey-green eyes, which caught the low Sun as she pushed a few strands of dark greasy hair back from her forehead. 'Where you from?'

'I . . . I come from Ryazan.'

'Well, you're in the right place, anyway.'

'How do you mean?'

'Ryazansky Station's just round the corner, ain't it? Everybody round here's from Ryazan.'

'Are you from Ryazan yourself?'

'Pronsk.'

'Oh!' said Konstantin. 'My mother came from Pronsk!'

'Who's that, then?'

'Her . . . Well, her maiden name was Yumasheva. Maria Ivanovna Yumasheva. Her parents had a workshop in Dolgoye, making barrels and –'

'Yeah, yeah, I know. Lord, you have come down in the world.' She hesitated, watching him. 'Rooms too much for you, are they? I seen you looking at the notices.'

'Yes, madam.'

'Well, there's no shortage of space. Harvest, ain't it? Everyone's got the hell out of here, and I can't say I blame them. Trouble is, no offence, but most people come off the train don't know their foot from their face. You can't blame people for trying their luck, can you?'

'No . . .'

'How much you got, then?'

'Three roubles, madam.'

'Run to four?'

Konstantin followed the washerwoman past an empty slaughterhouse and a tavern where a few drinkers were emerging into the waning heat, scratching at their sweat-soaked sheepskins, slapping at the mosquitoes. They passed through a gateway, formerly whitewashed, into a courtyard where there stood a wooden latrine – although this seemed to indicate a general area rather than anything specific, since it sat within a circle of morbid mould, innumerable flies and no fewer turds in various stages of decomposition, their stench so violent that Konstantin felt the tears coming to his eyes. On its far side, there stood a big dirty house, draped with lines of brightly coloured clothes, as if in perverse celebration. They crossed a type of causeway and arrived in a basement divided by whitewashed partitions, where the air was harsh with tobacco smoke and boiling cabbage, and a multitude of wasted, half-dressed people appeared from the crowded doorways – shouting, apparently to see if he could hear them.

Vera Valentinova lived in a room ten arshins long and five arshins wide. It had a high square window, sleeping boards around the walls and a stove shared with the neighbours, which was burning so fiercely that it could scarcely have been cooler in the oven. Above the fire, a pot of water was coming to the boil and condensation fell from the cracked, mould-smeared ceiling on to piles of stinking linen, a trough full of soapy water, a small bony girl, a naked toddler and an old soldier fashioning keys with hammer and anvil. In a corner cordoned off with further boards, Konstantin pulled off his shirt and his trousers and sank on to a thin straw mattress – the fleas bursting beneath him as he fell immediately asleep.

*

It was noon the following day when Konstantin entered a tall, arched door in the Chertkovsky Palace, and his nostrils filled with the rich, organic swell of books. After the torrid sunshine on Myasnitskaya Street, it took him several seconds before he was able to distinguish the library's deep-set windows, the ranks of shelves nearly twice his height, the desks where figures sat hunched over mysterious volumes, their faces stained green by the shades of kerosene lamps. Slipping past a mob of men around the librarian's counter, he found a ledger the size of a newspaper, which appeared to detail every book in the entire collection. He turned the pages slowly, reverently, his eyes travelling across titles on chemistry, history and mathematics, theology, philosophy and philology – all inscribed in the same firm hand. He took a scrap of paper from his pocket, multiplied the entries on one page by the total number of pages and came to the figure 27,950.

'Thirty-two thousand six hundred and twelve,' said a low, learned voice. 'Including the manuscripts.'

Looking up sharply, Konstantin found a librarian craning towards him, his long, bony fingers spread across the surface of the counter, his short grey beard almost brushing Konstantin's ear.

'I saw the ear trumpet,' he explained. 'May I offer any help?'

Cautiously, Konstantin took the instrument from his back.

'I . . .' he said. 'I'm looking for certain books about science, sir.'

'Are you a university student?'

'No . . .'

'It is, of course, much better to study in a library.'

'Do . . . you think so?'

'Certainly!' The librarian smiled, as if this were, after all, not a view to be taken too seriously. 'The university, alas, is an obsolete institution, a slave to industry, whose toys and trifles it considers to be mankind's highest imaginable achievement. It recognizes no authority, sets itself in judgement over our ancestors, over the prophets, even over God Himself!

'Of course, at present the library remains immature. It is unaware of its closeness to the Church and its inherent opposition to industry – and, yes, the university – but its day is approaching. The future lies in integration. When we have brought the words of the ancestors and the relics of the ancestors together beneath one roof, then we shall have made a crucial first step, and indeed, even now we are making preparations to move this entire library into the Rumyantsev Museum!'

Konstantin stared at the librarian in astonishment. He was a tall, ragged figure, his shirt plainly visible through a ruptured seam in his brown, shapeless jacket. Beneath his bald, vein-patterned head and black, thrusting eyebrows, he looked back at Konstantin with eyes as bright and ironic as a boy's.

'So,' he continued. 'Which books did you have in mind?'

'Well, sir . . . Please, do you have *The Principles of Chemistry* by Dmitri Mendeleev?'

'All four volumes.'

'And *Biographies of Distinguished Scientific Men* by François Arago?'

'All . . . eight volumes.' He glanced at the clock on the wall behind him. 'Unfortunately, we are obliged to close the library at three o'clock – an absurd rule – but if you would be good enough to appoint yourself a desk and make a list of your requests I shall assemble as many of your books as I can this afternoon, and any others will be waiting for you when we open in the morning.'

*

On his third morning in Moscow, at ten minutes to ten, Konstantin arrived at the Chertkovsky Library to commence a primary course in physics and mathematics. He sat on the step between the two bare-chested, cross-looking statues that projected from the sky-coloured wall and looked across the street at the cheerful signs of the grocers, fishmongers and ready-made clothiers that lined the opposite pavement. Smoking in their doorways, the shopkeepers were universally plumper than their counterparts in Vyatka – their faces pink, the napes of their necks clean-shaven. Above them, the city reached with confidence into the deepening sky: the domes of the churches exultant gold, the dense, lobed oak trees in the gardens of the mansions throwing softly stirring shadows across the trundling tramcars, the merchants' wives in their pearls and gaily coloured headscarves, the teams of hawkers selling ice cream, woodcock, dusters.

In the open street, three sunburnt peasants were kneeling in the hot sand, hammering cobbles with strong, discernible blows.

'Volodya,' announced a young man, loudly. He sat down beside Konstantin, extended an unclean hand and waited for him to lift his ear trumpet. 'I saw you yesterday, talking to Nikolai Fedorovich.'

'The . . . librarian?' asked Konstantin.

'Nikolai Fedorovich Fedorov is the Chief Cataloguer.'

'Oh . . .'

'I'm a student,' Volodya told him, 'which tends to elicit Nikolai Fedorovich's disapproval, but not all students are alike, are they?'

'I . . . I'm afraid I've never met a student before . . .'

'Not all students are alike,' Volodya confirmed. He took a cigarette from a pocket of his grubby, well-cut jacket, struck a match and considered Konstantin through his pince-nez.

'Nikolai Fedorovich . . . seems like a remarkable man,' said Konstantin, feeling that he ought to say something.

'You can have no idea how remarkable. He is the one man in Moscow to have called Tolstoy a fool to his face!'

'Tolstoy?' asked Konstantin, uncertainly.

'The count is a frequent visitor to the Chertkovsky Library. On a recent occasion, he found a book containing a list of every major in the Russian army and he told Nikolai Fedorovich that, were he the Chief Cataloguer, he would dispose of the entire collection save two dozen volumes. Well! Nikolai Fedorovich was not pleased. He informed him that every book contains the reminiscences of the ancestors, and that he was the greatest fool he had ever met!'

'Where . . . does Nikolai Fedorovich come from?'

'Well . . .' A queue of scholars and students was forming around them on the pavement, and Volodya seemed to appreciate the audience. He exhaled smoke into the sunlight. 'Some say that he was once a teacher in a town named Borovsk, in the district of Kaluga, and that he walked barefoot all the way to Moscow. Others say that he is the illegitimate son of Prince Gagarin, which would mean that he grew up in the district of Tambov, but if this is true he has certainly received no money from that direction. Nikolai Fedorovich has no possessions besides a trunk for a bed, a book for a pillow and a newspaper for a blanket. He lives in a room costing six roubles a month, if you can believe such a thing. He accepts a salary of only 498 roubles, since if he were to earn 500 roubles or more he would be obliged to perform jury service and he believes that no man has the right to pass judgement on any other!'

Volodya turned as the panelled doors of the library swung open.

'Come!' He stretched and rose. 'There is a spare desk next to my own!'

November 1873

'I've got a letter for you, madam,' said Vera Valentinova mysteriously, as Konstantin arrived at the well in the freezing gloom of an early-winter evening.

Around them, lights burnt in the tavern and the Church of St Yekaterina. A lantern swung from the box-seat of a big sledge grinding through the snow on Nemetskaya Street, its driver muffled to the eyes. Such was the heat in their room that the washerwoman rarely bothered to throw more than a shawl about her shoulders when she went to the well – although already she was shivering, and as she heaved her second pot to the hard ground she began to cough uncontrollably, the red blood blooming in her cheeks.

Slinging his ear trumpet across his back, Konstantin put the heavy yoke over his shoulders. He waited for Vera Valentinova to recover, then set out for the courtyard, where a couple of hefty, red-eyed men were dragging frozen carcasses from the slaughterhouse to a waiting sledge, among the yellow domes of urine that rose above the bullet turds in the dirty snow.

In the corridor, he seemed to smell the stench of wintering animals. He squeezed past drunkards in too-large boots, a mother and daughter assembling cigarettes out of paper cartridges and loose tobacco, a tailor squatting over an ancient greatcoat, the broad, short-legged women who seemed never to have anything better to do than smoke and paint their faces. Entering the room, he set the pots down gratefully near the stove. With a nod he greeted Sofia, the washerwoman's daughter, who was hanging clothes in tight, bright rows, and retired to his corner – wondering who could possibly have written to him here since he collected the monthly dispatches from his family at the post office near the library on Myasnitskaya Street.

His corner had been transformed during the past four months. By spending only ninety kopecks a month on bread, he had been able to save anything from five to ten roubles of his allowance, depending on his father's generosity, and his sliver of floor had been brought almost to the level of the cot by the tattered books he had bought in the Sukharev Market. On the partition, there hung a copy of the periodic table, which had cost him an extortionate rouble, while on the narrow shelf there stood several candle stumps, a kerosene burner, a tripod, a distorted retort stand, three blackened flasks and two ranks of bottles containing mercury, ethanol, iron filings, cobalt, magnesium and sundry other chemicals.

Speaking inaudibly, Vera Valentinova appeared above the eight groups of elements, a letter in her still-trembling hand.

The envelope was expensive, Konstantin could see that at once. It was pink and soft, and despite the stink of the steam and the linen he could smell its perfume, which told of carpets and silk-lined coats. Pushing his hair out of his eyes, he broke the seal and removed a short note written in a voluptuous hand, an address engraved along the top. He read it twice, and when he looked up he found that Vera Valentinova remained on the far side of the partition, framed by a lace-fringed tablecloth – her eyes narrow with interest.

'I ain't read it!' she insisted, as he lifted his ear trumpet.

'I . . . know,' said Konstantin.

'Even if my reading was any good, which it ain't, it ain't none of my business, is it?'

'Who is she?'

'Clarissa Emilovna?' The washerwoman frowned.

'Yes . . .'

'She's the daughter of Emil Ivanovich Tsindel.'

'Who's that?'

'Honestly, madam!' She rolled her eyes. 'The whole world just passes you by, don't it? Who do you think I do all my washing for, eh? Who do you think owns this bloody house? Emil Ivanovich Tsindel! The Emil Tsindel Factory? You've heard of that, surely?'

Konstantin shook his head.

'Emil Ivanovich Tsindel is the biggest manufacturer in Moscow! He's the Calico King! Christ alive, madam, Clarissa Emilovna's one of the richest heiresses in the whole bloody country!' She paused, expectantly. 'Come on! We're all of us waiting! Tell us! What does she want?'

'She . . . just wants to know who I am.'

'Why, then?'

'Well . . . She says that . . . She says that she's heard her servants talking about you and how you've got . . . Well, she says they say you've got a young alchemist living in your . . . house, and she wants to know if I can really make gold.'

'An alchemist!' Vera Valentinova exclaimed. She clapped her hands. 'Oh, that's priceless! Do you hear that, Viktor? An alchemist! Oh, that's made my day, that has!'

'Should . . . Should I write back to her, then?'

'Well, of course you should!'

'Would you be able to deliver it?'

The washerwoman stopped. Her smile subsided. 'All . . . All right,' she said, lowering her voice. 'I'm only doing it this once, mind. And keep it to yourself! You don't want her father finding out. He ain't exactly noted for his good nature.'

That night, Konstantin lay on his cot, composing his reply to the millionaire's daughter. Beyond the partition and the lines of the Tsindels' linen, the old soldier's hammer had fallen quiet and only Vera Valentinova's cough interrupted the silence. Through the subsiding steam, he could see the flame of a single candle reflected in the rotting plaster of the ceiling, and as he considered how to present himself in his best, most intellectual light, he could picture her sitting on her stool beside the stove, attending at last to clothes of her own, holding her needle between a thumb and two fingers, drawing the thread towards her with long, tired movements.

January 1874

One Saturday, Konstantin arrived at his desk to find a slim green book concealed among his normal textbooks. Its cover showed a train of cylindrical carriages pulled by a steam engine shaped like a bullet. At the top were the words *From the Earth to the Moon*, and at the bottom was the name 'Jules Verne'. Konstantin looked past Volodya, who was immersed in a political tract at the next-door desk, to the librarian's counter where Nikolai Fedorovich was entering the new acquisitions into the catalogue, writing intently, his lowered head reflecting a nearby chandelier. He watched him for several moments before he decided that the book must contain information relevant to his course, turned to the first chapter and started to read.

The book was, he assumed, some kind of fantasy, since if it were fact then even he would surely have heard of the enterprise before. It concerned an American organization called the Gun Club, which was devoted to the development of ever-greater pieces of artillery. With the end of the American Civil War, so the author explained, the purpose of the Gun Club had been called into question, and so its president, Impey Barbicane, had devised a new project to build a cannon big enough to hit the Moon. The idea alone was staggering in its audacity. The cannonball would need to achieve an initial velocity of 12,000 yards per second – fifteen times greater than the initial velocity of the greatest cannon currently in existence. The cannon Barbican proposed was 900 feet in length, nine feet in bore and six feet in thickness. This cyclopean machine would be located in Florida, on the Washington meridian, and it would be aimed in the exact direction of the Moon at its zenith.

Konstantin read with delight an account of the creation of the Solar System, when centrifugal forces triumphed over centripetal forces and the matter of the planets flew outwards from the Sun to assume their places in orbit, spinning themselves to create satellites. He laughed aloud at the casting of the cannon, when 68,000 tons of molten iron poured at once from 1,200 trapezoidal firebrick furnaces into a mould the size of a hollowed-out mountain, and when a Frenchman named Michel Ardan declared his intention to replace the cannonball with an aluminium shell fifteen feet tall in which he would travel as a passenger Konstantin felt an excitement so deep, so pervasive, that his hands began to shake and he had to weigh down the pages with a textbook to read on.

At last, observed by 5 million spectators from every quarter of the planet, a crowd that made even the Makaryev Fair seem like a family gathering, 400,000 pounds of gun cotton was detonated by electrical signal. A tower of fire rose half a mile into the air. The Earth trembled like an animal. A cyclone spread from the mouth of the cannon, felling the crowd like rye in the field, uprooting trees, sinking ships, disturbing the atmosphere so severely that the sky was swallowed by clouds. On the far shores of Africa, a sound like thunder was reported by the coloured natives of Liberia and Sierra Leone, and at his desk in the Chertkovsky Library Konstantin seemed to see the projectile streak out of the atmosphere, into the void: a speck of black against the Moon's dappled face.

*

The library, he realized suddenly, was empty. Even Volodya had vanished. He was sitting alone in the pool of light cast by his kerosene lamp, which was itself smoking, its fuel almost gone. Above the outlines of the desks and the hard, soundless floor, only two chandeliers continued to burn. He grabbed his cap, his exercise book and his pencil, and rose to his feet. He looked at the door, which appeared to be bolted, and turned to see Nikolai Fedorovich emerge from the shadows of the shelves, pushing a flight of steps, which he climbed to wind down another wick – the darkness rising from the narrow aisles, taking possession of the gold-traced ceiling.

'I'm sorry, sir,' said Konstantin. 'I . . .'

'Would you be good enough to help me?' the librarian asked, pleasantly.

'Yes . . . Yes, of course.'

They carried the wooden construction to the last chandelier, and when its flame was snuffed, a single lantern lit the gaping hall. Nikolai Fedorovich looked across the desks for any other trace of a spark, then he turned to a pillar of books, which threw a wavering shadow through the strata of smoke, across the walls and the sealed white shutters.

'Come!' he said, handing Konstantin several volumes.

He led the way down the nearest aisle, wings of shadow opening from the shelves, the lantern's light skidding across the red and green spines, through a small door, on to a staircase in which Konstantin could feel the librarian's slow, measured steps and at once fell into his rhythm. Here, the air was sharp and clean, the hidden winter pouring from the walls, the shadows of the stairs folding beneath them as they climbed. They arrived in a corridor, where the light glanced across crates full of journals and manuscripts, probed into rooms where the shelves were packed so tightly it seemed hardly possible that anyone could have squeezed between them. They climbed a second, tighter staircase, and came at last to a bare room bent beneath the pitching roof, where a kerosene lamp lit an icon of the Crucifixion. Nikolai Fedorovich added a birch log to a small iron stove and a couple of pine cones to the samovar, which seemed already to be simmering.

'So.' He sat down behind a desk piled wildly with papers and bookmarked books, lit a candle and gestured to a chair. 'What did you think?'

'About . . . the book?'

'About the book.'

'I thought . . . I thought it was prodigious, Nikolai Fedorovich.'

The librarian nodded, the shadows of his eyebrows quivering on his forehead. He poured thick brown tea into a pair of brown-stained cups and added sugar and boiling water.

'Just imagine!' he said abruptly, leaning towards the ear trumpet. 'Just imagine if the armies of the world were to come together in common purpose, to adapt their machinery to the conquest of gravity, the control and defeat of the blind forces of Nature! Just imagine if they were to turn their cannon from the horizontal to the vertical! After all, what is horizontality but the position of the animal, the position of the corpse, the position of submission to Nature? It is verticality that distinguishes man from his environment. When a child stands, is that not his first unnatural action, his first striving towards God? And think of the effect of this cannon! At once the sky floods with clouds, the barometer plummets and there is a rainstorm! I have read many accounts of how the use of artillery during the American Civil War was seen to provoke the clouds, just as people always said that the explosion of the Kremlin in 1812 brought rain. Can you imagine if the armies of the world were to aim their cannon not at the chests of peasants but at the clouds that mean their life and death? Well, then hunger would be no more!' The librarian drank, his forehead carved with concentration. 'There would be no further cause for conflict!'

Konstantin took his first sip of tea in six months, his thoughts stampeding.

'Tell me, Konstantin Eduardovich,' Nikolai Fedorovich went on, measured once again. 'What faults did you find in the Gun Club's project?'

'Well, Nikolai Fedorovich. I . . . Well, I do believe that such a project would be possible . . .'

'And why is that?'

'Well, according to Isaac Newton, it would be possible for a cannonball travelling at 11.2 kilometres per second to leave the Earth's gravitational field, which, I believe, equates to 12,000 yards per second, and there seems no reason why it would be impossible to create a large enough cannon. Whether the Gun Club's dimensions are correct, I really don't know. I would need to try and perform some calculations. But . . . As for any faults . . . Well, yes, I'm afraid I do think there is a problem with the concept of passengers. The Frenchman, Michel Ardan, is planning to make his home on the Moon, but it has long been established that there is no refraction of the stars at the edges of the Moon, which means that it has no gaseous envelope, and therefore that it probably has no water either since water would produce clouds of vapour, and besides . . . Well . . . I know that Impey Barbicane invents a series of wooden levels, which would collapse inside the projectile and help to absorb the shock of the explosion, but still the passengers would be struck by a wall of metal travelling at 40,000 kilometres per hour. I am afraid that they would simply be . . . flattened by their own weight.'

Across the desk, Nikolai Fedorovich was watching him closely, his eyes like lamps in the light of the candle.

'That is well spoken, Konstantin Eduardovich. Tell me. Do you have any ideas that might resolve this problem?'

'I . . . I'm afraid that I don't, Nikolai Fedorovich.'

'Anything might be helpful.'

'Well . . .' he said, after a moment. 'Well, I do wonder . . . I mean, if the Earth threw off the molecules of the Moon in the first place, and the Sun threw off the molecules of the planets, then perhaps there would be some way to . . . to follow their example? I mean, perhaps there might be some way to harness the Earth's centrifugal force?'

*

Konstantin emerged from a side door of the Chertkovsky Library, vital with tea, as alert and alive as the night itself. With payday in the factories, Myasnitskaya Street was a torrent of clean coats, polished boots and jackets shining with glass beads. For a moment he stood at the end of Furkasovsky Alley, peering at the stars behind the gas lamps, then he pushed his hands into the pockets of his sheepskin and set off south down Zlatoustinsky Lane, left on to Maroseyka Street, where the houses were taller and grander, and troikas flew at thirty kilometres per hour among the sledges and the revellers – the cockades of the coachmen fluttering, the hooves of the horses grinding sparks from the cobblestones. Behind their windows, he saw ladies in heavy cloaks, their coiffures splendid with jewels. In the doorways, where a little warmth leaked into the night, he saw men with torn shirts, shivering convulsively, their feet swaddled in strips of filthy linen. In his mind, he saw Moscow as a point on the planet, rotating through space at 960 kilometres per hour, and he imagined a craft thrown at such a velocity – out of this freezing darkness.

On the corner of Starosadsky Lane, Konstantin came to one of the three shops belonging to Emil Ivanovich Tsindel that he had found in central Moscow, and he looked past his scruffy, long-haired reflection in the window, past a wooden model of a full-breasted woman in a long black velvet dress, into a wealth of satin, silk and cotton – teeming with green leaves, pink flowers and shapes in swirling silver. He felt the heat from the glass through the acid-burnt holes in his thin trousers. He would, he knew, have a fresh letter from Clarissa Emilovna waiting for him at home, but still he took his exercise book from his pocket and read once again his letter from the previous evening, chuckling at her description of a starchy, snuff-taking aunt, smiling as she inquired in the mildest of terms if a normal mirror were not a more reliable addition to a telescope than a vessel full of mercury rotated around a vertical axis at a constant velocity to achieve a reflective paraboloid.

'Clarissa Emilovna!'

There was a moment before Konstantin realized that Volodya was peering over his shoulder, a thick scarf wrapped around his neck and a fox-fur hat spilling over his spectacles. Konstantin span, saw three other young men behind him on the pavement, hid the letter in his pocket.

'You devil, Konstantin!' Volodya laughed into his ear. 'And there was me thinking you were as pure as Nikolai Fedorovich!'

Konstantin looked past him, but he could see no means of flight. Reluctantly, he lifted his ear trumpet.

'That address . . .' Volodya repeated to himself, thoughtfully. He frowned, took a step backwards and looked with incredulity at the sign above the windows. 'No! Konstantin, tell me honestly now, is that a letter from Clarissa Emilovna Tsindela you have there? Honestly now!'

'No –'

'It is!' Volodya stared at him with open amazement. '*Mon ami!* With all respect to your charms, could you please explain how you have managed to attract the attention of one of the richest and most beautiful young women in Moscow? I mean, there are princes at court who attend the Tsindels' balls just to have a look at her!'

Konstantin slid his old felt boots on the frozen pine.

'Please, don't . . .' he murmured.

'Very well, very well . . .' Volodya put an emollient arm round his shoulders. His breath was rich with food and spirit. 'I'm sure it's from some other woman called Clarissa Emilovna, those most common of Russian names. It's gone! The thought is gone! However, it remains Tatyana's Day!' He turned to his friends, who replied with a faraway roar. 'It's the start of the student holidays, and you, my friend, are coming up to Truba, where we shall carouse and escape from our thoughts for some little time. My treat! After all, I will soon turn twenty and Milyutin has had his reforms! There'll be conscription for the lot of us! We must take our freedom while we have it!'

The night air seemed to fall several degrees as the sledge poured down Pokrovka Street, cutting through the holes in Konstantin's trousers, the loose weave of his homemade socks, the pockets of his sheepskin where his hands lay bare and freezing. Beside him, Volodya kept up an excitable dialogue with the *izvozchik*, waved to the skaters on Chisty Pond as if to personal friends. At regular intervals, he produced a tin flask from the lining of his coat, which he upended over his mouth and handed to Konstantin, who saw no choice but to do the same – gagging on the fierce, medicinal liquid.

'Where do you live!?' screamed the student at one point.

'Sunnikov House . . .' said Konstantin.

Volodya didn't seem to know where this was.

On their arrival in Trubnaya Square, Volodya tipped a few coins into the frozen claw of the driver's glove and fell into the snow outside a restaurant named The Hermitage, which

Konstantin had seen many times during his tours of the city – although tonight it was barely recognizable, its silk furnishings gone, its lavish carpets replaced with sodden sawdust and hordes of young, red-faced men. When a second sledge came ploughing towards them, the student greeted his companions as if he had not seen them in months. He took Konstantin's arm and, without warning, pulled him running across the icy square – heading north on to Tsvetnoy Boulevard, into a side street lined with *izvozchiki*, where, in spite of the cold, the doors to several shops and houses stood open in welcome.

Beneath a sign reading 'Fashion Shop', the five of them passed a scrawny man in a shabby black coat who was dozing on a sofa and, with more or less difficulty, climbed a staircase with a plush white carpet to a parlour hung with mirrors and countless lamps, arrayed with figurines in flamboyant poses. Near a marble fireplace sat a beardless boy with a violin and a bony old man at an upright piano. Across the parquet floor, soldiers and men in black bow ties were waltzing with ladies in yellow silk and dark blue velvet gowns – their faces painted, their bosoms so exposed that it was difficult to know where to look.

Possessed by a mood of unusual carelessness, Konstantin took a sweetmeat from a porcelain bowl on the sideboard. He watched the students remove their coats, hats and gloves, and disperse among the dancing couples, then he worked his way around the room to the musicians and set his hand on the lid of the piano, listening, feeling the music in the wood. As ever, it was the lower register that he could hear most clearly, but still he could just about follow the pianist's melody, his long, descending runs and moments of pause, which put Konstantin in mind of those ridges in the undulating Moscow streets where you would find yourself gazing across the rooftops, the treetops, the domes and the spires.

Konstantin saw the woman emerge from the crowd, her dark hair coiled with flowers, a smile imprinted on her handsome face. He watched her approach, tall, poised, not quite young, and when she arrived in front of him he fumbled for his ear trumpet, trying not to look down the plunging neck of her deep red gown.

'Oh!' she said, sharply. 'Are you one of the musicians?'

'Me?' asked Konstantin.

For a moment, the woman's forehead wore a quizzical frown, but then she seemed to remember herself and leant towards him, and he glanced involuntarily into the chasm between her fat pink breasts.

'Would you buy me a glass of porter?' she asked.

'Pardon?'

'A glass of porter?'

Konstantin looked at the woman in confusion. She had a voice he found impossible to place – aristocratic, but somehow lacking the insouciance of his aunt or his cousins – and although he knew that it was normal for wealthy women to paint their faces still he found it hard to see her eyes for their dark accentuation, and her lips seemed to bloom unnaturally, like a flower out of season.

'Your friend asked me to come and speak to you,' she explained.

'Why?' he asked.

'Don't you want to speak to me?'

Looking around the room, he saw Volodya vanish through a door in the corner in the company of a woman with bright orange hair. He fought battles in his mind, trying to understand why a woman of obvious prosperity should want someone to buy her a glass of beer, unless it was some aspect of social decorum, of which, of course, he knew nothing – although still he could hardly imagine Clarissa Emilovna asking him such a question, even if he had never actually met Clarissa Emilovna and knew her only through the confidences of her letters. For all he knew, in the privacy of their palaces all aristocrats behaved in this extraordinary manner.

The woman offered a soft, cool hand and led him past an officer in top boots and tight white trousers whose sword knocked against the inside of his knees and nearly made him fall. She set his arms around the back of her corset and put her own arms around his neck so that her breasts bulged against the lace of her chemise and the space between them vanished altogether. Konstantin smelt her harmonious fragrance. He felt a giddiness growing in his mind, and when she began to dance with sinuous movements of her hips he responded with movements of his own.

At length, there came a break in the rumbling of the piano and the couples parted, laughed, bowed to one another and turned to applaud the musicians. The woman ran her fingers down Konstantin's arm. With a secretive smile, she turned, tripped slightly on the hem of her dress and set out for the door in the corner – her bare neck white among the glaring lamps and mirrors, the velvet cascading in folds from her waist, sweeping the floor behind her.

Following dumbly, Konstantin arrived in a corridor of numerous doors and crimson wallpaper, where he was surprised to see a schoolgirl in uniform skip past him and vanish up a darkened staircase. He stepped aside for an ageing butler with a silver tray, then realized that he was delivering his bottle of spirit to the woman in the red dress, who was standing in the doorway of a room to the left.

The room was small, scented, lit by a lantern in a pink paper shade, which hung by a chain from the ceiling. Above a big feather bed, a tapestry depicted a bearded man in a spherical turban, pointed windows in the Tatar style and various women in startling states of undress. Konstantin watched as the woman set the tray on a bureau covered with a scarf, several visiting cards and an empty bonbonnière, poured two glasses, perched on the pink piqué counterpane and patted the space beside her.

'Your friend is very generous,' she observed as he sat down. She emptied her glass and waited for him to do the same.

'Is . . . Is he?' asked Konstantin.

The woman laughed abruptly, reached for the bottle, drained a second glass and heaved herself on to his knee.

Despite the layers of her dresses, Konstantin could feel her warm flesh spreading over the bones of his legs. He felt her weight, a confusing, fascinating heat that seemed to blend with the fire in his stomach until it enveloped his entire body.

'How old are you?' she asked huskily, her lips to his ear.

'Sixteen . . .'

'I'm sixteen too.'

'Really?' He looked at her doubtfully.

'Do you like to have the light on?' she continued.

'I . . . wouldn't be able to see without the light on,' said Konstantin.

With the lightest pressure of her ring-clad fingers, the woman pushed him backwards on to the bed. He saw the flame in the lantern above him. He felt her tug at the waistband of his trousers, leaving him naked to his spot-patterned thighs. Frozen with astonishment, he saw her seek her balance, then lift her long red gown and several levels of flounced petticoats to reveal pointed shoes, a pair of lace-trimmed stockings with scarlet garters, an angle of hair between broad, white, naked hips.

He looked at the lantern as she straddled him. He did not

dare to look at her – although he felt her every movement with a fearful intensity, and soon even the flame seemed to be shivering to her rhythm, sending pulses of pink across the pink-stained ceiling. He watched the flame's reflection in the polished copper tank. He watched the air that shimmered at the mouth of the glass chimney, where water vapour mingled with carbon dioxide.

In time, the woman doubled forwards and began to move more vigorously. Her face loomed above him, smothered in shadow. The ribs of her corset were sharp against his stomach. Her breasts grazed the straggling hairs on his neck and his chin, his grubby shirt, the fleshless contours of his collarbone. Beyond her sealed eyes and her swinging earrings, her hair was surrounded by a halo of light.

Her flowers, he saw, were not flowers after all, but fashioned out of sheets of coloured paper.

*

Konstantin stumbled back along the side street, past gaping doors and shivering drivers who cast him indifferent glances. On the corner with Tsvetnoy Boulevard, he turned to see the man in the black coat standing on the pavement, smoking, calling to a woman who leant from the upstairs window of one of the houses opposite. He skirted the crowds outside a raucous tavern and, his soft boots slithering on the slippery street, set out north on the central promenade where the lonely gas lamps burnt above benches lost beneath the snow.

On the bleak expanse of the Garden Ring, the houses vanished behind gaunt trees, leafless shrubberies, tall iron gates. Konstantin thought of Clarissa Emilovna in her lace-trimmed nightdress and her clean white sheets. He longed to be lying beside her, his ear to her lips, listening to her tales of nurses,

German tutors, French governesses, poets and fancy-dress balls, explaining to her once again that he would one day become a great man, as great as any man who had ever lived. Crossing the wide, empty thoroughfares of Samotechnaya Street, he found himself in a deserted park. He passed beneath a snow-draped goddess, a garland of roses pressed to her bare stone bosom, and he only stopped, breathing irregularly, when he was standing in the middle of a skate-scratched pond – the houses and the streetlamps lost among the treetops behind him.

The craft arrived unbidden in Konstantin's mind. There was, he realized suddenly, no need to try to harness the centrifugal force of the Earth. He could simply create a centrifugal force of his own. With each passing instant, he perceived more of the brilliance of his idea. If he were to revolve a pendulum with sufficient velocity, he would be able to propel a vessel independent of all other forces. If he were to revolve a pair of pendulums, he would be able to moderate their respective velocities and use them to travel in any direction he chose, while by means of gradual acceleration he would achieve the painless ascent that would elude a cannonball of any variety. He stood on the ice, his head turned backwards, his eyes on the averted face of the sliver Moon, and even now he seemed to feel the weight lifting from his feet. He seemed to see through portholes in a thick iron hull the fires of Moscow receding beneath him, the stars approaching like falling snow, the Sun emerging from the vault of the planet – its heat like rapture, spreading through his emaciated limbs, the bones of his ribcage, the moonlit angles of his face.

*

In the dirty snow of Petrovsky Boulevard, the dirty light of dawn, Konstantin passed the bolted face of a fourth shop belonging to Emil Ivanovich Tsindel and emerged once again beneath the muted gas lamps and the snow-lined oak trees of Trubnaya Square. Outside The Hermitage, a few haggard waiters were piling the broken furniture and vomit-caked sawdust of the previous evening on a bonfire on the exposed cobbles where a handful of vagrants held shivering hands towards the stifled flames. Tottering on feet in which he had lost all sensation, Konstantin joined their meagre circle. He felt the fire's heat through the scrubby hair on his cheeks.

'Th . . . Thank you,' he stammered, as an old man in a pair of tattered galoshes picked the broken glass from a strip of beef and handed it to him.

With the gathering light, the carts of the Sunday bird market were creeping up Rozhdestvensky Boulevard, their drivers motionless, their horses climbing with slowly swinging heads. One by one, the traders found their places in a line along the western side of the square. They brought smells of hay and recent warmth. They assembled themselves before walls of homemade cages full of cocks and ducks, mangy chickens and lean, hungry pigeons, siskins and skylarks, blue tits and blackbirds, thrushes and goldfinches that flickered their impotent wings.

The first collectors were frowning and haggling, warming their hands on steaming cups of tea, by the time that Konstantin was able once more to use his fingers. Squatting on the stones beside the dwindling bonfire, he took a pencil from his pocket. He lay his exercise book on his knees and began the letter that he had been composing all night.

He told Clarissa Emilovna all about his spacecraft. He told her that it would, in an instant, remove her from Moscow, from the iron routines of which she wrote to him daily, and transport her at velocities unimaginable even to the most visionary manufacturers of air balloons and steam locomotives to any part of the Universe that she might care to visit. It could, he told her, take them together. It could take them to the spas of the Black Sea, or the palaces of England where the queen would receive them with amazement and delight. It could take them to the Moon. It could take them on a tour around the Sun.

February 1874

It was the third day of Butter Week when Vera Valentinova collapsed as she entered their room, dropped her heavy wicker basket and remained where she fell, her shoulders shaking, her red hands pressed to her narrow face. Kneeling on his mattress, Konstantin watched as the old soldier, Viktor, lifted her carefully and sat her on the stool beside the stove. He glanced down to see his mixture of copper oxide and sulphuric acid resolve itself into a deep blue copper sulphate solution – as *The Principles of Chemistry* had predicted. With a breath, he extinguished the kerosene burner and hurried into the room.

'Vera?' he asked. 'Vera, are you all right?'

Hobbling to the window, Sofia took a handful of snow from the sill and stirred it into a cup of water.

'Do I . . . ?' The washerwoman turned on him with blood-tangled eyes, the colour burning in her cheeks. 'Do I look like I've got a bloody letter? Eh? Do I? Do I look like a messenger to you? Or a bloody post-boy?'

'No,' said Konstantin, quickly. 'No, I came to see if you were all right –'

'By all that's holy! What did I do to deserve you? Or your Mademoiselle Clarissa Emilovna, and her stuck-up bloody maid, who looks at me like I'm so much dirt on her shiny little shoe! You ain't going to get no more letters! Got it? She ain't sending them and I ain't bringing them and there's a bloody end to it!'

Konstantin felt the strength failing in his legs.

'Wh . . . What do you mean?'

'Her bloody father's found out about it, ain't he? Someone's gone and told him there's some strange man writing secret letters to his precious daughter and he ain't pleased about it. He really ain't pleased about it! And when Emil Ivanovich Tsindel ain't pleased about something –'

Beyond the bell of his ear trumpet, Konstantin saw her face contort with another wave of coughing. He moved aside so that Sofia could hold the cup to her lips. On the floor beside them, the laundry basket lay broken open, revealing the gown of a tall young woman – its silver pleated skirts tapering to a waist so narrow that he might have enclosed it with his hands, its bust small and elegant between neat sleeves of brightly coloured jewels.

'I'm . . . I'm sorry, madam . . .' Vera Valentinova put her hands to her eyes, her thin lips trembling, pale and taut. 'I can't believe that I could have been so stupid. I ought to have stopped it. Here's . . . Here's me with a husband in the army, and three children to feed, and not a kopeck I don't make out of slaving myself half to death. The only people knew anything about them letters was her and her maid and the people in this room, and that's it, and however you look at it, it comes back to me, don't it? Me and my children, and no one to look after us . . . I don't even know why they gave me any laundry! I'm just waiting for someone to tell me I ain't got no work no more and I can clear out of here while I'm about it, and I'm trying to think what the hell I'm going to do, and the choices ain't very pleasant I can tell you!' She reached into the pocket of her skirt and produced the folded, wax-sealed sheet of coarse-grained paper that he had given her that afternoon. 'He's sending her to Petersburg, madam. It's all been arranged. You just got to forget all about her!'

*

Ten minutes later, Konstantin arrived outside in the courtyard, but for once, instead of turning right towards the slaughterhouse, he turned left between the mounds of frozen urine and entered a lesser-used alleyway where a distant gas lamp told the wooden walls from the trampled ground. He passed a yard piled with snow-capped birch logs, framed by cattle pens, chicken coops and a giant house made entirely of glass – its roof bare and arching, its smells of unnatural growth colouring the winter air.

It was snowing, gently. On Gavrikovsky Lane, Konstantin saw a three-storey mansion, its unshuttered windows dazzling with filament bulbs such as Alexander Nikolaievich Lodygin had demonstrated in St Petersburg the previous year. The light poured across the icy street, eclipsing the gas lamps, slicing a pyramid from the weaving snow. On the steps, as if in daylight, he saw no fewer than thirty footmen, dressed alternately in livery of silver and gold. Inside, it seemed, some manner of ball was underway. Through the nearest window, he saw men and women in masks of glorious colour. He saw flowers in bushes and arbours. He saw wines, soups, pies, cheeses, cakes and, borne on the shoulders of four large servants, what appeared to be an entire pig encased in pastry.

Konstantin shivered in his wretched sheepskin. From the north, a black, jewel-spangled equipage arrived with its four black horses, and a lady in a tiara and a long black cape ascended the steps to exchange kisses with a full-bearded man who appeared from among the revellers to greet her. Behind them, momentarily, Konstantin thought he saw a tall young woman in a crimson gown, a flash of pale shoulders, a flood of golden hair. Alone on the pavement, he heard the faint impression of an orchestra. He stood with his letter in his hand and watched the Sun-defying light of the great house distort and refract, its angles appear to open, its walls appear to bow.

*

Konstantin lay as he had lain for the past five days, curled with her letters in the hollow of his cot, his knees to his chest, conscious dimly that someone was hammering on the boards of the partition. It took a crippling effort to open his eyes and pull himself upright, to dip a corner of his blanket in the cup of water on the shelf and wipe at the hair that clung like mould to his chin, his lip and his cheeks. It was normal these days for him to suffer nosebleeds. They were just another thing that he had had to learn to tolerate, like his black-bread diet, like his hair, which now fell almost to his mouth, like the holes in his trousers and the lice perusing tirelessly through his underwear, feeding on his spot-blemished limbs.

Beyond the bright, indifferent lines of the laundry, Nikolai Fedorovich was sitting on the stool at the mouth of the stove. As if out of nowhere, he produced a slab of chocolate in golden paper, which he proceeded to divide – handing a piece to Vera Valentinova, to her son and two daughters, even to Viktor, who ate cautiously with his few yellow teeth, like he had never tasted chocolate in his life. The librarian turned to stir a tin flask in the embers at the edge of the fire, then received from the boy a little wooden soldier, which he held to the candlelight, admiring its rifle, its peeling paint of white, red and blue.

'Konstantin Eduardovich!' he said warmly, looking up. 'I was afraid that you were ill.'

Konstantin stood bent over his ear trumpet, his eyes on the dark, wet floor.

'Your presence has been missed in the library.'

'I've . . . not been well,' he murmured.

'Well, I hope you will not think me presumptuous, but it happened that one of the students brought me some soup. It looks rather good. Cabbage and potato. Like you, I incline towards cold food as a rule, but I thought that you might care to share it?'

Covering his hand with the sleeve of his well-patched coat, Nikolai Fedorovich collected the flask from the fire and emptied it into Vera Valentinova's wooden bowl, which he set on the table beside the trough – beads of hemp oil trembling on its yellow-green surface. He waited for Konstantin to sit down, crossed himself and indicated for him to take the first spoonful.

'No butter,' he apologized. 'Such is Lent.'

Konstantin ate mechanically, the hot soup fierce and unfamiliar in his shrunken stomach.

'Thank you, Nikolai Fedorovich,' he said, at last.

'It is a pleasure, Konstantin Eduardovich. Tell me, are you feeling strong enough to face the outside air?'

'I . . . Well . . .'

'There is something I would very much like to show you.'

Konstantin followed the librarian into the terrible night, where the fires of the city burnt in the low clouds and a north wind fled down Nemetskaya Street, carrying snow which bit his face, discovered the holes in his trousers and his sheepskin so that even before they crossed the frozen ocean around the Red Gate he was shivering uncontrollably. Nikolai Fedorovich walked with a loping gait, his old leather boots beating time on the pavements, his shoulders hunched forwards so that he had to lift his chin, and with every streetlamp his eyes disappeared into the shadows of his forehead. From time to time, he looked down at Konstantin, tramping beside him, his arms enclosing his narrow belly, and they had almost reached the Chertkovsky Palace when he stopped abruptly at one of the big department stores, pushed through a door into a glass-covered passage, removed his hat and ushered Konstantin into a small shop framed by a pair of spherical gas lamps.

Konstantin smelt the refined smells of leather, starch and linen. He felt the heat in the carpet through the thin soles of his felt boots. He saw an assistant in a pair of gold-rimmed spectacles bow to each of them in turn, and vanish through a door between a pair of glass-fronted cabinets to return a moment later holding a long brown greatcoat.

'Try that,' the librarian instructed, bending to his ear.

Removing his ear trumpet, Konstantin did as he was told. He pushed his arms into the sleeves and found the coat comfortable even over his sheepskin – the warmth of the shop in its wadding, its double seams and calico lining.

'Does it fit?'

Konstantin frowned.

Nikolai Fedorovich removed a bundle of paper roubles from a trouser pocket, counted out several and handed them to the assistant.

'Nikolai Fedorovich!' Konstantin protested, recovering his ear trumpet.

'Konstantin Eduardovich,' said the librarian, calmly. 'As Chief Cataloguer of the Chertkovsky Library –'

'Nikolai –'

'As Chief Cataloguer of the Chertkovsky Library,' he insisted, 'I receive an annual income of 498 roubles, of which I require approximately one third. The rest of it is of no consequence to me whatsoever. However, I have a coat which keeps me warm, and I have not spilt reagents on my trousers.'

Discreetly, the assistant disappeared.

'But, Nikolai –'

'My dear fellow,' he interrupted. 'Good things happen some-times, as well as bad things. You must accept the one, and it only makes sense to accept the other. I admit that I am not the foremost authority on matters of the heart, but I have heard enough from your landlady and that wretched student Vladimir Mikhailovich, to whom the army is entirely welcome, to learn that fate has not been kind to you of late. So, within the mysterious schematics of the Universe, consider the coat as some fractional redress, and if you wish to show your gratitude to me then do no more than consider my advice, since I am not entirely without experience of the world. Indeed, as a teacher in Borovsk, I was even engaged to be married.'

The librarian stood tall, serious, heavy-browed, the blue veins tangled on the white expanse of his forehead.

'Yes, Nikolai Fedorovich . . .' said Konstantin, eventually.

'I should make it clear,' Nikolai Fedorovich continued, 'that I am opposed neither to marriage nor reproduction. Without them, mankind would suffer extinction before it had managed to achieve its purpose, which would be an incomparable disaster. I do, however, believe that urban culture has fallen into a cult of femininity, a worship of the sexual instinct, which is profoundly humiliating to the human intellect. You have only to look around this department store to see how industry and technology have come into its thrall, elevating luxury goods to a status contending with, even supplanting, religion, and reducing man, who was made in the image of God, to the level of a prettified animal. Now, I appreciate that to resist this splendour of putrefaction is no small matter in itself, but for those of us engaged in a life of chastity, whether by accident or design, there is a still-more important choice to make: the choice between negative chastity and positive chastity. The former is merely abstinence. The latter is the redirection of sexual energy towards knowledge and action!'

The night did not seem quite so fearsome in the heavy greatcoat, which kept out the air and even, to some measure, the darkness, and as Konstantin followed the librarian beneath the fire-cut walls of the Kremlin he looked with some little interest at the figures working in the immensity of Red Square – smashing with iron bars the great ice mountains of Butter Week, their sledges of ice and graceful, facing slopes, piling into pyramids the ships and the limbs of the swings, the gilded horses of the roundabouts, the ruins of the booths that had lately sold tortoises, carpets, sweets, toy monkeys, the galleries, pillars and balconies of the palatial wooden theatres that stood in places still half intact.

In the runner-torn snow of Alexander Garden, Pashkov House rose above them like a cathedral: five colossal levels of columns and balustrades, windows beyond counting, wings which alone were the size of any mansion in Vyatka. Konstantin and Nikolai Fedorovich crossed a courtyard and entered a door as tall as that of a stable. They climbed a flight of marble steps between portraits of barefaced generals and guitar-strumming maidens, and arrived in a room where a two-storey house might have been erected without any inconvenience to the men in overalls who were hanging wallpaper from tall, slender ladders. Ahead of them, Konstantin saw halls with chessboard floors, golden chandeliers and shelves of books in their hundreds of thousands. Together, they walked among glass cases of Old Slavonic manuscripts, letters, diaries, into reading rooms with galleries and desks in private alcoves, through long, well-lit chambers where Konstantin saw a bull with wings and a human head, a tenth-century mosaic of the Saviour, a golden cross from Byzantium, a rare chromate of lead from Siberia, a gigantic quartz crystal from Yekaterinburg, the entire skeleton of a mammoth.

'Tell me,' called Nikolai Fedorovich, as they emerged in a narrow stairwell. He waited for the ear trumpet. 'Did you have any further thoughts about harnessing the planet's centrifugal force?'

'I . . . I did, Nikolai Fedorovich,' Konstantin admitted. 'But . . . I'm afraid it was an elementary mistake.'

The librarian took a candle from one of the bright brass brackets. 'No matter.' He smiled. 'We shall use the conventional means of ascent.'

The staircase led to a small, octagonal room on the very summit of the palace, where the heat of the combined words and relics of the ancestors kept eight tall, arched windows free of ice, and Konstantin turned from the five shrinking levels of a church in the west, to the two frozen arches of the Moskva in the south, to the muscular spires and louring palaces of the Kremlin in the east.

'In the West,' Nikolai Fedorovich told him, as he inspected the wind-scattered smoke of the hidden fires in Red Square, 'the celebration of Easter, the great feast and the great deed, has almost disappeared. It is only in Russia that it retains its importance, that Christ, the prototype of all mankind, suffering and risen again, is granted his true and rightful position . . .'

Konstantin found his eyes straying north across the barren trees and the half-seen roofs. He felt the weakness in his limbs, peered into the distance – as if the filament bulbs on Gavrikovsky Lane might have been visible even from here.

'Yet even in Russia,' the librarian continued, in the same reflective tone, 'we face the threat of a pornocratic future. That is to say, in our age of unthought there is every danger that men will abandon the theological beliefs of their fathers and come to see themselves purely from a zoological perspective, and that, by seeing themselves as animals, they will become animals, forgetting their history, living in the present, like cattle. In such a future, religion would come to be seen as no more than an infantile superstition, an unnecessary appendage belonging to an earlier period of mankind's existence.'

Through the warm air, Konstantin felt the freezing fingers of the gale reaching into the cracks around the windows, heard its distant scream as it clutched and tore at the snow-hunched roofs, the arrogant façades of the great city.

'God made man in His own image!' declared Nikolai Fedorovich suddenly, turning to him, the candle burning in his eyes. 'Did He make man passive, supine, horizontal? No! He made him active, creative, vertical! Had man only recognized this fact in the very beginning then he need never have left paradise! Had he exercised his potential, controlled Nature as God controlled Nature, as God Himself enjoined him, then the world would have remained perfect. But he abused his freedom, he forgot his sacred duty, and in his Fall he lost his position as Nature's master and instead he became Nature's slave!

'There is, Konstantin Eduardovich,' he continued, 'only one true course for humanity! We must join together to turn the blind and unfree forces of Nature, acting both within and without us, into the tools of our own liberation – for what is Nature but the organ of death, the organ of our own destruction? Of course, we must learn to defeat storms and droughts, disease and insect infestation, but our task will not be complete until we have defeated the very essence of Nature, which is death itself – until we have assembled the particles of every ancestor who has ever lived and resuscitated each one in his turn, back to the very father of our species, that all might become whole and perfect and immortal, as the scriptures describe! Perhaps this idea seems startling to you? Perhaps the challenge seems so great as to be insurmountable? But, I repeat, man was made in the image of God! The only limit to his ability is the limit of his own imagination! You may tell me that the resources of the Earth cannot hope to provide for such a multitude of immortal beings, but I reply that the human imagination can overcome any obstacle. The Earth does not exist in isolation! It is open in every direction! We have only to find the means to transcend the limits of our globe, and we will be able to colonize other planets as we would colonize the lands across any ocean – adapting ourselves through the wonders of technology until we are able to inhabit even the most inhospitable environments! It is our duty, Konstantin Eduardovich, to rise above this cradle of our infancy, to become a heavenly force, masters of every world in the vastness of the Universe!'

Lyubov

August 1878

Konstantin rolled his cartwheel north beneath the full-bodied poplars of Zatinnaya Street, his ear trumpet swinging from his shoulders, two long-legged chickens in a pair of wicker cages on his back. At the junction with Voznesenskaya Street, a woman holding a broom watched him with amusement, becoming laughter, but he paid her no more attention than he paid the mumbling carts in their haloes of dust, the stunted tower of the Church of St Yekaterina, the short-sighted windows of the old, familiar houses. Even in the heavy August heat, Ryazan seemed pitiful, contaminated: a naked asteroid, trapped in the orbit of Moscow. Had any of his friends remained in the city, he might have made some effort to moderate his appearance, trimmed the lank brown hair that fell across his shoulders, worn his spectacles the right way up in public – even if the arms were too long and he had to push them continually back up his beak of a nose. But in the four months since he had returned from Vyatka he alone had avoided military conscription – having demonstrated his ability to blow air out of his ears – and anybody else had long since been siphoned away by the unstoppable advance of the railway.

Scaling the embankment, Konstantin followed the tracks above the fringes of the city, the listing huts with their meagre plots of cabbage and cucumber, the tangled wormwood and the red-hipped dog roses on the waste ground. His wheel bumped rhythmically over the sleepers. As he passed the single, uncovered platform of the station, he felt the eyes of the sweltering travellers, the peasant women selling milk, kvass, cold chicken and boiled eggs. He saw the smoke of the morning train at Lagerny, felt its weight, its movement in the rails. But he knew that three kilometres separated the two stations, and that the train never exceeded fifty kilometres per hour, and he was descending a path among the scrubby trees on the far side of the little Pokrovka River by the time that a 2-4-0 came rumbling past in a storm of steam – the fireman heaving birch logs into the firebox, the driver leaning round the backless cab, distantly sounding his whistle.

At the tall, log-built watermill, Konstantin inserted the cart-wheel's broken length of axle into a brick-lined hole in the dusty yard. He tied the cages to either side of the wheel's upper face and gave it a spin to check that they were level. Lean, sun-brown, a carter in a sheepskin emerged from the mill's grumbling darkness, leant against the door frame and lit a tree-root pipe. Behind him came the miller himself: a big, bald-headed, flour-stained man whose son Konstantin taught mathematics two hours a week in exchange for his use of the mill for his experiments.

'Morning, Chairman!' the miller barked, his long beard grazing his ear.

'Good morning, Ilya Valeryevich,' said Konstantin. He retrieved his ear trumpet.

'How much for a ride?'

'Would . . . you like to volunteer?'

The miller laughed and clapped him on the back.

'Fifteen minutes do you?' he asked. 'We've got a few sacks to be getting along with.'

As Ilya Valeryevich went to close the sluice in the mill race, Konstantin pushed his way through the nettles round the pond, swept aside the scum and the goose feathers and filled his hands with water to pour over the axle. He took a rope from a hook on the meal floor, and when the cogs and the stones had fallen silent he slung it round the broad vertical shaft between the spur wheel and the wallower, fed it into a groove in the underside of the hub and pulled it tight.

Konstantin took from his pocket the watch left to him by his brother Ignat, who had succumbed to typhus in Vyatka two years earlier. He watched as the breastshot waterwheel began once more to turn – beads of sunlight flinging from its radiant blades. He watched the rope bite, and as the cartwheel gained angular velocity he observed the behaviour of the chickens, who looked around them sharply, claws scrabbling as they slithered towards the outside walls of their cages and soon lay upright, passing the same point within a single second – their combs horizontal, their feathers frantic, their yellow beaks open in alarm.

'Eighty-one revolutions per minute!' Konstantin exclaimed. He grinned and the carter, already shaking with laughter, turned to slap the miller's hand. 'Eighty-one! With a radius of rotation of 75 centimetres, that means they are experiencing a fivefold increase in weight, and look at them! They're fine! They're absolutely fine!'

February 1880

'Now,' said Konstantin. He wiped from the blackboard a jumble of fractions and decimals, and a picture of a cake divided into slices. 'For the rest of the morning, we are going to consider the Solar System. So, what is the Solar System? Can anyone tell me?'

He turned on his platform and looked across the classroom, where twenty-four children looked back at him from their eight long desks – poised on puberty in grey skirts and trousers, linen shirts tied at the waist and headscarves tied around the chin.

'Pyotr?'

One boy lowered his hand, approached the front in grubby felt boots.

'Is it . . . the Sun and the planets, sir?' he asked loudly, as the teacher cupped his ear.

'The Sun and the planets!' Konstantin agreed. He smelt the boy's must of pigs and sheep. 'Just so! Yes, as you all know, we live on the Earth, which is a ball of rock spinning around the fiery inferno of the Sun. But the Earth is not alone. Indeed, to the best of our knowledge, the Sun is surrounded by at least 119 other rocks, of which eight are large enough to be considered planets . . .

'So. Who can tell me the names of any of the planets?'

He turned, wrote 'THE PLANETS' at the top of the blackboard, felt four pairs of feet in the classroom's worn, sagging floorboards.

'Mars?' said Sonia.

'Venus,' said Marta.

'Jupiter!' said Pyotr.

'Saturn?' asked Ilya.

'Excellent!' Konstantin straightened up, added the names of the planets in order to the board. 'Which gives us five, including the Earth, and I'm sure that you will recognize the others when I tell you. Nearest to the Sun we have Mercury, the smallest planet in the Solar System, a mere one-seventeenth the size of the Earth. You see? Fractions get everywhere! Beyond Saturn, we have cold, faraway Uranus, which is eighty-two times larger than our own planet, and then, way out on the edge of inter-stellar space, we have even colder, even further-away Neptune, which lies at an average distance of 4,320 million versts from the Sun and was discovered as recently as 1846 . . .'

He removed his new, correctly oriented spectacles, polished them on his handkerchief, replaced them on his nose and went to stand at the window near the stove – watching the west wind steal the smoke from the chimneys of Borovsk, stirring up storms on its huddled roofs. He clicked his tongue and removed from a bag beneath his chair a large black medicine ball, two wizened apples, two pickled cherries, a dried pea and a rye grain, which he arranged along the edge of his desk.

'So,' he continued, considering the classroom. 'As I'm always telling you, there is little point in learning facts and figures unless you understand what they mean, but to understand the Sun and the planets is no easy matter since they are so very much larger than anything we know in our day-to-day lives. In due course, we will talk about each of the planets in more detail, but first I would like you to think about the relative sizes of the Sun and the Earth. The Earth is big, as you know. Indeed, if you were to tie a belt around the Earth's middle, that belt would be 42,750 versts long! But if the Earth is big, then the Sun is enormous! Enormous! If you wanted to tie a belt around the Sun it would need to be a staggering 4,658,500 versts long!

That's 109 times longer! For the moment, then, I would like you to think of the Sun as this medicine ball. Here it is! The Sun! If this is the Sun, then what is the Earth? Not an apple. That would be Jupiter. Not a cherry. That would be Uranus or Neptune. No, our own great, glorious Earth would be ... a pea!'

Konstantin paused, smiling at the laughter that spread around the room.

'A pea!' he repeated, enthusiastically. 'While the Moon, Diana, Queen of the Night, would be a miserable rye grain! And if you think that it's difficult to imagine the sizes of the planets, then consider the distances between them!'

*

There were the usual drunkards around the tavern on the far side of Rozhdestvensky Street: bearded men, red-cheeked women in kaftans, long skirts and sleeveless dresses that would have been two hundred years out of fashion even in Nikolai Fedorovich's day. They were shouting, laughing, a couple of them punching one another repeatedly in the face, but they paused to watch the young teacher of mathematics, science and geometry narrow his eyes against the wind, wait for a troika parading the dowry of some rich family – a feather bed, a dining table, a dozen geese, a set of brass lanterns – and take up a position in the middle of the open street.

'Volunteers!' said Konstantin, when the children were assembled in front of him.

Several gloves rose among the scarves, pink faces and sheepskin coats.

'Nikolai?' He handed the medicine ball to a boy in a red woollen cap, which reminded him distantly of Ignat. 'And one more, if you please?'

This time he chose a quiet girl with deep-set eyes, who was standing near the back of the group and raised her glove only when most of the others had done the same.

'Isidora?' He handed her the pea. 'Now, your job is particularly important. That is the Earth you have there, after all. What I would like you to do is to take 180 good long steps in the direction of the marketplace, then turn towards us and lift the pea right up in the air so that we can all see it. Is that clear?'

'Yes, sir,' she said, almost inaudibly.

'Good girl!'

Konstantin watched her stride away along the tracks of the troika, shrinking between the one-storey wooden houses whose tin fire-insurance badges were the only indication that this haven of Old Believers existed in the age of steamers and railways. She veered to one side when a dog erupted from its kennel to the limit of its rope, and she paused to curtsey to a woman carrying a few scraps of straw to her cow, but at length she crossed the junction with Myshkovskaya Street, stopped and turned: a piece of punctuation beneath the wild, grey-white clouds.

Konstantin indicated to Nikolai to lift the medicine ball, then peered towards the pea in the invisible hand of the barely visible girl.

'And there you have it!' he declared, with satisfaction. 'If this is the Sun and that is the Earth, then there is the distance between the two of them. One hundred and forty million versts! A good long way, is it not?'

*

Shortly after two o'clock, Konstantin returned to the classroom, having forgotten his satchel, and set out once more down the slope towards the Protva – following a path between snow-drowned houses with bellying walls. He stopped on the bank among the thrashing willows, leant against a fence to strap his skates over his old leather boots and pushed himself on to the ice. By throwing his weight from one foot to the other, he gathered speed quickly, and as he passed a fisherman hunched above a hole and a struggling chub, he opened his umbrella and felt the wind swell inside the taut black fabric – bending his knees, leaning backwards to maintain his balance. Beyond the shelter of the bank, a gale tore out of the small town, across the narrow river and the snowy water meadows, and it was a matter of seconds before he swung his umbrella to the left, angling his skates so that the blades bit the ice, and steered a course towards the meander – his short beard shivering, his neat hair fluttering between the collar of his greatcoat and his homburg hat.

He bounded up the path towards Chistyakovskaya Street, reversing his own faint footprints, greeting an old woman who was dropping rocks into her well and watched him so warily that he might have been a Selenite. Near the grubby little Church of the Protection of the Blessed Virgin, he came to an angular wooden house, two storeys tall, which wore a blanket of snow on its pitched plank roof and openwork carving on its eaves and its windows. Kicking his boots against a derelict sledge, he hurried into the warm air of the hallway, where, beneath a mirror framed in white and peeling gilt, he found a crate with his name and address written neatly on the lid.

Konstantin's apartment sat directly above his landlord's kitchen: a pair of airy rooms whose three large windows looked down the hill towards the frozen river and the fringes of the pine forest that gave the town its name. Dropping his hat, coat and scarf on an armchair with silky red upholstery, he set the crate carefully among the jumble of papers, chemicals and scientific equipment on his desk. He prised off the lid, scattering sawdust, just as he noticed three logs burning in the open fire, and, turning towards his bedroom, nearly collided with his landlord's daughter: a firmly built girl two months his junior, her dense black hair pulled back from a pale, square face, her grey eyes sweeping the neatly swept floorboards.

He started, rummaged for his ear trumpet.

'Varvara Yevgrafovna . . .' he faltered.

'Konstantin Eduardovich . . . I . . . didn't think you would be back so soon.'

'I hurried . . . You lit my fire. Thank you.' His thoughts returned to the crate. 'Perhaps . . . Perhaps you would like to see my purchase?'

'Yes . . . Very much.'

Busily, Konstantin assembled his optical microscope. He slotted the lens and the eyepiece into the objective turret, attached them to the stand and fitted a mirror into the bracket beneath the stage. He set the instrument on the windowsill, and for once had reason to resent the girl's astonishing cleanliness as he searched the cracks of the floor for the body of an insect. It was several moments before he found a long-dead honeybee, which he blew clean of dust, lay on a slide and pushed into place. He sat his spectacles on his head, adjusted the knobs and exclaimed as he saw a pair of goggling compound eyes staring back at him from a forest of hairs – white with the light of winter.

'There!' he said, excitedly. 'Look at that! Look!'

He watched the girl bend forwards, her skirts describing the arch of her hips, her single plait falling past the shoulder of her crisp white blouse. For a second or two, she peered into the eyepiece, then she gasped, drew her head back sharply and crossed herself with two fingers.

'Dear Lord!' she managed. 'It's . . .'

'Beautiful!' said Konstantin. 'Isn't it? Beautiful!'

*

'You see, Konstantin Eduardovich,' said Yevgraf Nikolaievich Sokolov, as the two men sat together that evening in the companionable warmth of the dining-room fire. He poured himself another brandy. 'Boyarina Morozova was an influential woman. She was a lady-in-waiting to Tsarina Maria Ilyinichna and the sister-in-law of Boris Ivanovich Morozov, Lord Protector to Tsar Alexei and the second-wealthiest Russian of his day. But she was also a penitent of Avvakum Petrov, Protopope of the Kazan Cathedral on Red Square. You know it, no doubt? Avvakum was one of the fiercest opponents to the reforms introduced by Patriarch Nikon in 1652. That is to say, certain amendments to the wording of the creed and the spelling of the word "Jesus", the use of three fingers rather than two in the Sign of the Cross . . . Well, it is a lengthy list, and may seem pedantic to a scientific man like yourself, but if you consider that these things constitute not merely the medium of worship but the very matter of the Divine then you will understand that they are a subject of the gravest importance.'

Yevgraf Nikolaievich applied himself to the poker. A small, ragged man in late-middle age, he had cheeks scarred with ruptured blood vessels and a still-red moustache, whose tips erupted like flames from the body of his long grey beard. As a priest in the Yedinoveriye Church, the mildest of compromises between the Orthodox Church and the Old Believers, he was, in the eyes of most of the town's population, as much a heretic as Konstantin himself.

'So, you see,' he continued, as the fire boiled and flared in the draught from the chimney, 'Boyarina Morozova became one of the most prominent members of the Old Believers' movement. She even took monastic vows. Well, at first, Tsar Alexei attempted to persuade her of her error, but when, in 1671, she failed to attend his wedding to Natalya Kirillovna on the pretext of illness, he had her arrested, and she began the first of a series of imprisonments, which culminated in a cellar of the St Paphnutius Monastery, here in Borovsk, where she starved to death in 1675. To her followers, of course, she became a martyr, which explains the town's significance to the Old Belief.'

'And what became of Avvakum?' asked Konstantin.

'And you a teacher, Konstantin Eduardovich!' Yevgraf Nikolaievich laughed, drained his glass, reached for his bottle. 'It is as well that you are not a teacher of history! Well, Avvakum visited the cellars of St Paphnutius himself in the 1660s – although he managed to survive until 1682, when he was burnt at the stake in a town named Pustozyorsk in the Arctic Circle. Death by fire was not, alas, an unusual fate. Avvakum himself maintained that self-immolators flew to the light like moths. In those days it was not uncommon for entire communities of Old Believers to lock themselves in their churches and burn them to the ground. Of course, they believed that the Kingdom of Evil was upon them, as many of them still do – hence their refusal to recognize any innovations subsequent to the reforms, from the eating of potatoes to the smoking of tobacco. To their minds, they were imminently to be resurrected, as the patristic writings tell us, neither old nor young, neither male nor female, but in a state of humanity free of the sexual impulse, as we were before the Fall.'

Soft as a shadow, Varvara Yevgrafovna entered the room from the kitchen. She collected the plates and the soup bowls, folded the tablecloth and placed them together on the old-fashioned mahogany sideboard. She blew up the samovar and refreshed the sweet black tea in Konstantin's chipped china cup.

'Thank you, Varvara Yevgrafovna,' said Konstantin.

With a bow, the girl retired to the corner, where she removed the cat from her chair, opened her sewing box and resumed work on an antimacassar, which she was embroidering with a horseman, a monastery and a wealth of brightly coloured birds.

'An excellent girl!' observed Yevgraf Nikolaievich, who appeared to believe that she had left the room. His words were beginning to run together. 'What I would do without her I cannot imagine. Since the death of her mother, she has kept this house single-handedly. Single-handedly, mind! If I had money for a servant . . . If I had money . . . She deserves better, Konstantin Eduardovich. She is an excellent girl, good and dutiful, and healthy! On my word, she has not suffered a day's illness in her life. And she's clever too! She plays the harp beautifully and her knowledge of the gospel rivals my own!'

March 1880

Konstantin sat in the red armchair from his apartment, spread his shoulders, felt the hard springs beneath his thighs. He tucked his scarf into the collar of his greatcoat, then tugged on the halyard so that the sail flapped and fluttered in the first good wind to come to Borovsk in several days. A strong white triangle sewn by Varvara Yevgrafovna out of scraps from Protopov's factory on Podvysokovskaya Street, it shone in the late-winter sunshine, and when it reached the masthead he pushed the boom firmly to his right and watched the runners from Yevgraf Nikolaievich's old sledge turn in the fine, thin snow.

Around the Protva, the fields, roofs and gardens of Borovsk were lunar in their beauty. The sunlight glanced between the windows of the houses and the domes of the Cathedral of the Intercession of the Virgin, the threadbare contours of the armchair and the luminous banks where the long shadows of the birch trees lay as faint as ghosts. At first, Konstantin eased out the sheet, spilling wind to test the strength of the mast and the sail, turning the bar at his feet so that the ice-skate rudder carved a sweeping line behind him, but he was barely halfway across the river before he swung the rudder firmly to the left and saw ahead of him the clear, straight kilometre of ice that stretched north-east out of the town.

By the time the last houses of Borisoglebskaya Street had dwindled on the north bank, the armchair was travelling as fast as a locomotive. Konstantin flew past a peasant on a cantering horse. He took his first meander with the well-spread runners slithering, steering south so that the sail jibed and the end of the boom just missed his nose, and he left the muffled roofs and the glinting cupolas of the village of Roshcha at a broad reach, chuckling with pleasure, tucking his hands into his pockets, hunching his shoulders to conceal his ears from the fierce, Arctic air. As he sped between the open fields, he tried to calculate how long it would take him to weave his way back up the river, which was nowhere more than fifty metres wide, but with every upturned fishing boat, every fisherman's hut buried neck-deep on a long, thin island, every crowd of willows whose churning branches appeared to roar, urgent with existence, he longed to see more, and even as he described a torturous zigzag beneath St Paphnutius Monastery, its teetering bell towers and medieval walls rising improbably from the forest, he could scarcely wait for the next turn to the south.

At last, the river turned so purposefully south that the return journey seemed almost insuperable, and Konstantin lowered the sail and slowed to a halt at the mouth of a stream. As far as he could see there was nothing but the river, the ice-white Sun, the pathless forest. Pushing himself to his feet, he tasted the cold, clean air, flapped his arms to restore their circulation. He examined the skate at the end of the left runner, the tiller lines that ran either side of the roped-down armchair, then he looked again at the walls of the pines, here as tall as the river was wide, the snowflakes, alight, ephemeral, tumbling from the tips of their thin black branches.

With his first steps on to the stream, Konstantin felt the wind die almost completely. He saw the shadows melt, reveal contortions of snow, drifts of incalculable construction unseen before by human eyes. He stepped over roots, the twin impressions of his heel and sole extending behind him. He scaled a sculpture of a waterfall, glittering in the last light from the river. As he pushed into the forest he saw a few dim scraps of colour among the great pillar trunks, and he emerged in a little clearing where the stream met its source and the low, snow-bowed branches were decorated with fragments of material.

Konstantin watched the water gasping through a small round hole in the ice – dilating on the surface as if the Earth had been pierced in its frozen integrity, as if the pulse of the planet was exposed. Crouching down, he waited for the water and filled his hands, and as he drank he felt a shock simultaneously in all part of his body, as if he had grasped the terminals of an electrical machine. Involuntarily, he sucked in air. He gasped. He arched his back and turned the discs of his spectacles from the ground's breathless silence to the fine green treetops, where the lines of sunlight danced like the absent birds.

April 1880

'Let us imagine that this room is on the Moon,' said Konstantin to Varvara Yevgrafovna, who had that evening brought her antimacassar to the fireside. 'Let us say that you have fallen asleep, and wake suddenly. What do you see? Well, at first, nothing might strike you as unusual. It would take you some moments to notice that the clock's pendulum is swinging at a sixth of its normal velocity, as if it has grown six times in length. Intrigued, you rise to your feet, and it is only then you realize that all is very far from normal. Pushing your hands against the arms of the chair, you all but fly across the floor and stand uncertainly some arshins distant, wondering perhaps whether you are still dreaming. Of course, all this is to imagine that the house has somehow been hermetically sealed, since there is almost certainly no atmosphere on the Moon . . .'

Beside them, Yevgraf Nikolaievich snored distinctly, sank another centimetre in his sagging armchair, but the girl did not so much as glance in his direction. In the faint light from the unshuttered window, her eyes were as silver as the cross around her neck.

'Go on,' she prompted.

'Well, perhaps in your befuddlement you take hold of the dresser. Good Lord, you have the strength of Hercules! You meant simply to steady yourself, but you find that you can lift it easily – though it is a full fifty poods in weight! You see, the Moon has a very much smaller volume than the Earth, so its gravitational force is proportionately slight. By retrieving the spring balance from the kitchen, you discover soon enough that your strength is really no greater than normal, that you can deliver the same five-pood force as you would on Earth, but still what wonders, what feats are not now within your powers! You are able to move lightly, unencumbered, your body possessing a mere sixth of its previous weight –'

'A little like swimming?' suggested Varvara Yevgrafovna.

'Indeed!' said Konstantin, keenly. 'The lightness must be a little like being immersed in water – although, of course, there would be no resistant medium. I am unable to swim myself, I'm afraid, so I don't speak as much of an authority.'

'You never learnt to swim, Konstantin Eduardovich?'

'Alas, no . . .'

The girl tutted, smiled. 'So, what would I see if I looked out of the window?'

Lowering the long, shining shaft of his ear trumpet, he offered his hand, and so she set down her sewing and rose to her feet, her own hand small and strong. He led the way across the floorboards, past the sideboard and the large, oval table, and they stood together between the curtains, observing the hillside sunk beneath the year's last snow, pink in the day's dying light: the snow-trimmed alder and willow trees on the riverbanks, the smoke rising straight from the chimneys on Nizhnaya Street to dissipate high in the freezing air.

Above the forest, the Moon alone was perfectly white.

'Outside,' said Konstantin, 'you would encounter a scene of absolute silence. Without an atmosphere, the stars would not scintillate as they do here on Earth. They would appear more like the stars on the dome of a church, or silver nails hammered into the heavens, and they would move almost imperceptibly since the axial rotation of the Moon is twenty-eight times slower than the axial rotation of the Earth. Compared to the Moon, the Sahara Desert is a paradise! In the Sahara, there are date palms, oases of life. On the Moon, there is nothing: no wind, no clouds, no snow, no lakes, no water of any kind. There are no subtleties of colour, simply mountains of bare, jagged rock, their lines unsoftened by ice or waves. Indeed, the only colour would belong to the Earth itself.'

Varvara Yevgrafovna shivered in the cold air pouring from the big panes, pulled her shawl around her shoulders.

'Tell me about the Earth,' she said, stretching to his ear.

'The Earth! The Earth would be magnificent! Well, by day it would seem something like a milk-white cloud in the funereal sky, but at night it would be three or four times larger than the Moon appears to us and some fifty times brighter – quite bright enough to read by. The seas and continents would appear like a picture behind the pale blue glass of the ether. At once, you would see the entirety of Africa, Europe, the Indian Ocean, the expanses of Asia – even the Gobi Desert. You would see great swathes of cloud, the shining caps of the Arctic and Antarctic, the snowy peaks of the Alps, the Himalayas and the Caucasus Mountains. Terrestrial eclipses would be frequent and majestic. On such occasions, the stars would appear in an abundance beyond our imaginings, while the Earth would seem a great, dark circle in the deep red corona of its atmosphere – the colour infusing the rocks all around us!'

'And if we went outside?'

'Outside . . .' Konstantin echoed. He continued to stare through their faint, pale reflections. 'Yes. It would be possible to venture outside, but only if we were dressed in some kind of suit, like a membrane enclosing the body, protecting us from the lack of atmospheric pressure and the excesses of heat and cold, equipped with vessels to supply us with oxygen and food – although with the relative weakness of lunar gravity these need not be particularly burdensome. But if we were to go outside, well! What couldn't we do! At first, to gain momentum, we would have to lean forwards, like a pair of horses pulling a heavy cart, but then there would be no need even to walk. We could simply travel by enormous leaps, like a frog or a grasshopper! We could vault crevasses and bound up the flanks of mountains! With a little practice, we would be able to perform somersaults with ease! And if we were to run, well, we would run as fast as a racehorse! Since one lunar day lasts as long as fifteen terrestrial days we would need only to move at fourteen and a half versts per hour and we would be able to remain abreast of the Sun, so that the lunar night need never fall! If we had a rifle, we would be able to fire a bullet a full seventy versts vertically upwards, almost into space! Just imagine that, Varvara Yevgrafovna! How easy space travel would be for a Selenite!'

Beside him, the girl was watching him intently, her face soft and young, her eyes open, Moon-coloured.

'Do you think, then, that there might be people on the Moon?' she asked.

Her smell was warm and fresh and alive.

Konstantin smiled and looked back at the Moon's brightening arch, the gathering stars. 'I must admit, Varvara Yevgrafovna, it is a matter to which I have given a good deal of thought. After all, do we not see life on our own planet in all manner of conditions? In salt water and fresh, in the air, in the soil, on the tops of the mountains and deep in the ocean where the pressure is a hundred times greater than the pressure on its surface. Life is miraculous, endlessly inventive, so how can I consider life on the Moon to be impossible? What does an organism actually need to survive? Well, it needs heat. It needs oxygen, but from a scientific point of view it is not impossible that oxygen could be provided by special internal organs, able to photosynthesize like the green parts of plants here on the

Earth. It is, I believe, possible that a creature could exist on the Moon if it combined the characteristics of plant and animal in a single, wonderful whole. Consider the radiolarian, a unicellular animal that lives on the surface of the ocean and contains chlorophyll besides its other, amoeboid characteristics. Since it is established that land animals have adapted from animals that emerged from the sea, is it not possible that a lunar animal might have adapted from an organism like a radiolarian? Might there not exist an entity effectively independent, reprocessing its own oxygen and waste materials by means of photosynthesis and requiring only sunlight for survival? Take our own planet by way of comparison. The Earth is isolated in space. Nothing enters our atmosphere of any significance besides the heat of the Sun, and yet life, through the harmony of its multitudinous organisms, uses the same materials endlessly, over and over again. If you can imagine in miniature what on the Earth we see in the large, then perhaps you have imagined a Selenite: a creature with a skin impermeable to every kind of fluid and gas, a creature with no external orifices, perhaps possessing beautiful emerald wings able to turn automatically to the Sun, through which carbon dioxide would pass absorbed in the blood to be enriched with oxygen, hydrocarbons and certain nitrogenous compounds. For such a creature, these wings would be an orchard, a garden, a field, a cattle-shed! They would mean that he need never experience thirst, or hunger, or indigestion! Consider those trees on Earth that can survive a thousand years in the face of winds, parasites – all of the massed and hostile forces of Nature! Then consider a creature perfect in his isolation! If a tree can survive a thousand years, then a creature of this kind could survive almost indefinitely! Effectively, he would be an immortal!'

He turned to Varvara Yevgrafovna, who continued to watch

him, her arms around her shoulders, her fine lips gathered in a distant laughter.

'And tell me, Konstantin Eduardovich,' she asked, once more rising on her toes. 'Would you be happy like that?'

May 1880

The entire population of Borovsk seemed to come outside with the warm spring evenings, when even the Sun showed no inclination to sleep until it was nearly ten o'clock and lingered above the westerly forest like a child trying not to be dispatched to bed. Along Medinskaya Street, the old people dragged benches from the dark, stinking holes of their kitchens and sat among the buttercups, the wandering chickens and the shadows of the small-leaved lime trees, talking with eerie expressions which suggested tales of goblins, evil spirits and the nightly departure of the dead from their graves. Their hands on their sticks, they watched Konstantin and Varvara Yevgrafovna emerge from their tall, crooked house. They followed them with yellow eyes – shaking their heads at the shamelessness of the younger generations.

Above the flat fields in the valley, the blossom of the apple trees, the plums and cherries cloaked the hillside in pink and white. Their scent made its harmony with the deep, damp song of the soil. Konstantin and Varvara Yevgrafovna descended Krutitskaya Street between hedges purple with flowering lilac. They joined the track beside the high, brown river, where a pair of horses was dragging a sledge of dung through the liquid mud. Among the trees at the edge of a flax field, a circle of women was dancing to the music of a young man with an accordion – orbiting a birch tree as if it were the Sun. The women wore intricately patterned dresses, red-and-white headscarves, garlands of bellflowers and wild pinks. Around them, a crowd was passing bottles, clapping to the accelerating metre. The women danced with twinkling steps, turning counterclockwise, and as they span faster so their dresses revealed their old-fashioned linen petticoats, their slim white ankles. One woman's headscarf came off altogether so that her long bronze plait flew horizontally outwards, her large eyes laughing, her big breasts lifting with each step, pressing against her loose white blouse, and Konstantin watched with growing fascination until he felt a tug on the sleeve of his jacket.

Beneath the thin, unfolding leaves of a willow tree, they pushed a grubby punt down the bank into the churning Protva. Konstantin looked with concern at a crack in one side, but Varvara Yevgrafovna mimed urgent paddling, and so he held out his hand to help her aboard, and once she was settled in the prow he positioned himself in the stern. He pushed them uncertainly up the channel between the bank and an island impenetrable with rising reeds and tangled driftwood, bent almost double, feeling with the pole for the solid bed beneath the soft mud, and when they came to the central current he angled the boat towards the opposite bank and allowed them to drift the length of a wooded peninsula before, at a signal from the girl, he swung them awkwardly into its eddy, the water already slopping round their feet – guiding them north until all trace of the town, the smoking tanneries and the sunlit domes of the Cathedral of the Intercession of the Virgin, had disappeared.

On a pale, muddy beach, Konstantin turned the punt over. He sat on the hull, swatting mosquitoes, admiring the pink and yellow flowers of the rosebay and the St John's wort, which covered the ground beneath the flood-ringed trees.

'This is nice,' he admitted, after a minute.

'I used to come down here with my mother.' Varvara Yevgrafovna looked with pleasure at the gently moving water. 'I really wasn't sure if it would still be here. The willows are pretty thick on the peninsula, I suppose, but some years the banks and the islands change completely. Sometimes the river floods so badly you can only see the treetops poking from the water, waving like rushes. If it weren't for the trees you wouldn't even know where it was! I remember, one year, the river rose all the way up to Nizhnaya Street. I used to have some friends who lived there, and to stay above the water they had to pull up the floorboards and balance them on the furniture. They spent the whole night sitting in a line, with the water still rising and the icebergs battering the shutters!'

'Your mother wouldn't swim, though, surely?' said Konstantin.

'Oh, yes . . . The thing about this place is that it's perfectly secret. The woods are thick all the way back up to the fields, and the peninsula gets more and more covered with brambles as the summer goes on. No one can see you unless they paddle up that channel from the river. I suppose people must row up here sometimes to go fishing or blackberrying, but I've never seen them. My mother lived in Likhvin when she was a girl. She used to swim in the Oka all through the summer, and she didn't really see why she should stop just because she was a grown-up.'

'What did your father think?'

'I don't suppose he ever knew.'

'So . . .' He hesitated. 'What do I do?'

'Well, this is a good place to learn,' said Varvara Yevgrafovna, brightly. 'There's no real current, and you shouldn't get much out of your depth. Swimming's all about confidence. Anyone can stay afloat if they think they can stay afloat, but if you want to swim properly you should start by cupping your hands and drawing them out to either side. Like this.' She demonstrated. 'And as you pull your hands backwards, kick out your legs like a frog, so the soles of your feet push against the water. You see?' She smiled and gestured at the pool. 'Don't worry. You just need to get started, and then do lots of practice.'

'We . . . I might need to find another boat if I'm going to do that.'

'You're prevaricating,' she said, firmly.

His back to the girl, Konstantin stood on a patch of dry grass, removed his spectacles, his ear trumpet, his jacket, his boots, his socks, his trousers and finally his shirt, which he draped together over a branch. Pale and ungainly in his long white drawers, he trod through the mud and sank his feet in the bitter water. He winced, and were he not being observed he would certainly have retreated to the bank to wait for some sunny afternoon in July, but even though his feet were numb and aching he continued to wade forwards until his waist was framed by the dark, turning water, the trembling reflections of the drooping leaves and the cirrus clouds. For a moment, he waited, breathing through his teeth, his arms round his bony chest, but he knew that if he remained there he would probably catch a chill, and so he bent his knees, crossed himself and slipped into the river.

Konstantin swallowed water, thrashed his arms as if drowning. He kicked out wildly, but when he touched the bottom he felt his own lightness and, remembering the girl's instructions, he began clumsily to pull himself forwards, splashing but remaining afloat until he encountered the mud of the opposite bank.

Turning in triumph, Konstantin could see no trace of Varvara Yevgrafovna. In a wash of panic, he pushed his wet hair out of his eyes, looked from the punt to the matted trees and flowers, into the intervening water. Several moments passed before he noticed that a skirt and blouse were hanging from the branch beside his own clothes, and he looked up the river to see the girl swimming calmly with the eddy – her black hair tapering to a trailing plait, her shoulders rising rhythmically, pale and naked.

August 1880

It took three assaults on the door of a high log house, cream-painted, curiously devoid of windows, before the priest of the Orthodox Church of the Nativity of the Virgin emerged in his snuff-coloured cassock, his cheeks riven with wrinkles, his eyelids fluttering. Behind him, among the levels of tobacco smoke, the empty bottles and the still-burning candles, an auburn-headed boy lay face down in a game of 'fools'. The priest looked from Konstantin in his fresh, pressed suit, his steel-rimmed spectacles and homburg hat to Varvara Yevgrafovna in her long black skirt and lace-edged blouse, her twin plaits making one another's acquaintance on her shoulder. Blinking with pain and confusion, he peered at the brilliant trunks of the birch trees that surrounded the little village of Roshcha – their pointed leaves stirring and turning in the early-morning sunlight.

'What . . . time is it?' he asked, at last.

'It is seven o'clock, Sergei Mikhailovich,' said Konstantin.

'Seven o'clock!' The priest put his hands to his grizzled temples. 'What do you want, Konstantin Eduardovich? Are you here to torment me?'

'We should like to be married.'

'At seven o'clock in the morning! Who gets married at seven o'clock in the morning? Tell me that! Who gets married in the summer, even? Nobody! It is contrary to the laws of God and Nature!' He turned to the bride, who stood silently beside Konstantin. 'Varya, you are here under duress, are you not?'

Varvara Yevgrafovna shook her head.

'Then . . .' He looked down the hill towards the Protva and

the shadow-striped fields, across the low stone wall into the cemetery, where a few calves and sheep were grazing steadily. 'Then where, pray, is your congregation? Where is your father, Varya? Where is your best man, Konstantin Eduardovich? You cannot marry without a best man! It's unheard of!'

Konstantin lowered his ear trumpet and took a sheaf of roubles from the pocket of his trousers.

'We would just like to marry quietly, Sergei Mikhailovich. I . . . wonder if perhaps your friend would be good enough to help?'

In the great, empty nave, Konstantin and Varvara Yevgrafovna stood before the five moulded storeys of the iconostasis, where the saints in their flamboyant raiments bowed their heads to the Virgin and Child. The couple held candles white and blazing in their left hands, so close to one another that Konstantin could feel the intimate pressure of the girl's shoulder in the muscle of his arm. Behind them, the boy had composed himself sufficiently to sit a pair of gilt, velvet-brimmed crowns on their heads. Above them, the sallow, bearded face of Christ looked down from a sky of motionless stars. Konstantin watched the priest in his stole and his crimson, gold-embroidered phelonion, his breathing laboured as he read from a battered black Bible. The previous summer he had been obliged to study Old Slavonic for his teaching examination, and at one point he identified a passage from John – the wedding at Cana, where Jesus turned water into wine – but such was the solemnity of the occasion that it seemed inappropriate to use his ear trumpet, and for the most part he heard nothing but a series of grunts and moans.

*

Konstantin sat in the armchair in his apartment, his eyes on the window, his head on the completed antimacassar, which comprised his entire dowry. In the light of the low evening Sun, he felt himself elevated, suspended by unknown forces above the shallow valley, the dusty roofs, the blazing fields of yellow rye. For long, unmoving minutes, he watched the mist condense over the Protva: a luminous ribbon, which ran among the willows as if the spirit of the river, its animus, had been revealed by some mysterious process of refraction.

At length, Konstantin removed his spectacles and placed them on the desk. In the timbers of the house, he felt the drunken celebrations of Yevgraf Nikolaievich and his scant congregation. He crossed the floorboards to the door of the bedroom, where the shutters were closed and, in the little light from the icon lamp, he could see no more than the shape of his wife: the ingress of her waist, the swell of her hips, the sudden division of her legs. She was standing near the curtains, untying her hair, which retained a certain kink as it fell across her shoulders, her upper arms, her naked breasts, which he discerned more clearly as the seconds passed: pale, erect, dark towards the tips. Had he been able to hear her reply, he might have complimented her on her appearance or made some joke to relieve his tension, but instead he stood motionless in the doorway, separated from her by the corner of the iron-framed bed. He watched as if hypnotized as she turned towards him her tapering back and the dark globes of her buttocks, reached for the icon of Vasily the Blessed and turned the saint to face the wall.

August 1881

A year elapsed.

On the first Monday morning of the autumn term, Konstantin arrived in his classroom to find those few children in attendance standing at their desks, smiling and clapping their hands. After two sleepless nights, he seemed to have acquired a preternatural sensitivity. At the back of the room, the big, colourful map of Russia and Little Russia possessed a fresh depth, a brilliance. Between the windows and the whitewashed walls, the elongated impressions of the window frames were dazzling with sparks. Even the applause sounded bright, precise, almost loud.

He went to the window and inspected the tawny schoolyard, the late-summer splendour of the limes and the birch trees, the intricate golden clouds. He set down his satchel on his desk at the front of the room, and from his shoulder he removed a white silken bundle whose microscopic stitching appeared to shine with a light of its own.

'It's a nice day,' said Konstantin, finally. 'Isn't it a nice day?'

The children nodded.

'Thank you for your congratulations . . . I . . . You must excuse me, I . . . I have had rather an unusual weekend . . . The timing of the school year has, perhaps, not been ideal.' He considered these seven of his pupils not required by their parents to gather firewood or lead their horses to pasture, then realized that he was staring at the low-topped boots of the boy at the nearest desk. 'Well . . . It doesn't seem right to begin the school programme with so few of you present . . . I think, perhaps . . . Shall . . . Shall we go outside?'

In the shade of an apple tree said to have been planted by an inmate of the prison that had stood there fifty years earlier, the three girls and four boys assembled a square of benches. They huddled together so that he would be able to hear them, eyed the handful of apples that remained among the downy, serrated leaves.

'I thought,' Konstantin started, 'that I would tell you about buoyancy . . . You have all seen buoyancy in action, haven't you? You've all seen logs drifting down the river, or smoke floating in the air. Buoyancy can be described as a vertical, upwards pressure. Essentially, the rule is that if a body is heavier than its surrounding medium – that is to say, air or water – then it will sink, because its weight is greater than its buoyancy. If a body is exactly as heavy as its surrounding medium then it will float where it is, because its weight counterbalances its buoyancy. And if a body is lighter than its surrounding medium then the buoyancy will prevail, which is the reason why a boat will float or an air balloon will rise. You see?'

The children nodded, tentatively.

'Now.' He took a small metal bowl from his satchel, lit a twist of newspaper with a match and fed the fire, first with twigs, then with larger scraps of wood. 'Most of you have probably never seen an air balloon and I myself have never seen an air balloon on any scale, but in the future this technology will certainly provide an important method of transport. As yet, it is the only form of human flight to have enjoyed any success. As long ago as 1783, two French brothers named Montgolfier had the idea to build a large silk sphere with a hole at the bottom. Beneath this hole they hung a sort of boat containing a fire to heat the air inside, and since warm air is lighter than cold air their balloon rose . . .' He gestured upwards, through the branches of the apple tree, into the breeze, the clouds, the temperamental sunlight. 'It rose to a height of 2,800 arshins!'

Ilya raised his hand, so the teacher cupped his ear.

'Did they die, sir?'

'Well, on that occasion they did not travel in the boat themselves. But it was not long until they began to experiment with human passengers, and, since that time, aëronauts have risen to altitudes that even the Montgolfiers could scarcely have imagined. In 1862, a pair of Englishmen, James Glaisher and Henry Coxwell, took a balloon full of coal gas to an altitude of 16,700 arshins. That's 4,200 arshins higher than Mount Everest, the tallest mountain in the world! At such a height, the air is so thin that it is almost impossible to breathe. It is bitterly cold and so dry that paper becomes crumpled, as if it has been placed before a fire! At such a height, the sky above you is almost as dark as the sky at night, and the Earth beneath you curves distinctly – as if you are looking down from space!'

When the fire was established, Konstantin filled the bowl with pieces of charcoal and unfolded his balloon. He instructed the children to stand in a circle, to hold it in place, and once he had attached the bowl to a special wire cradle, as if witnessing a miracle he watched it swell, pitch in the breeze, rise past the apple tree, past the chimneys of the surrounding houses, and hang from its tether at a level with the domes of the cathedral.

'You see?' said Konstantin, in a distant voice. 'The contents of the balloon are lighter than the surrounding medium.' He looked at his pupils, who stood with their heads and caps tipped backwards, watching the white wavering spot with unconcealed amazement. He tied the string to his bench and sat back down, closing his eyes as he tried to organize his thoughts. 'So . . .' He looked up to see faces in the windows of the other classrooms.

'Can anybody tell me? Is it possible to take a balloon all the way to the Moon?'

There was some indecision, but one girl shook her head.

'No? Why not, Marta?'

'Because . . . there's no air there, sir.'

'That is one reason, yes,' said the teacher. 'Certainly a balloon cannot be lighter than nothing. But, ultimately . . .' He picked up a stone and allowed it to fall back into the dust. 'Ultimately, the problem is gravity. Buoyancy can lift us high into the atmosphere, but it will never allow us to pass into space. We are all of us gravity's prisoners!'

'Is it not possible to go into space, then?' asked Marta, loudly.

'Oh, it is possible, but only by moving at the most incredible velocity! You see . . . Let me see . . . Try to picture the Earth in your minds: an enormous ball suspended in space. Yes? Now, imagine that you are standing on the top of a mountain so tall that it pokes right through the atmosphere. You pick up a stone and throw it horizontally. What happens? Well, of course, your stone travels forwards and it falls, due to the force of gravity. For a while, it follows a curving line, but then it falls vertically, and in the end it hits the ground. Right? Well, two hundred years ago, a scientist named Isaac Newton calculated that any object thrown horizontally will fall five metres with every second that it remains in flight. He also noted that we are standing on a ball, which, of course, has a curve of its own. Indeed, from a horizontal line the surface of the Earth descends at a rate of five metres every eight kilometres. You see?' He drew a picture in the dust. 'Now then. Imagine again that you are standing on your mountaintop and that you throw a stone horizontally away from you, but that this time you throw your stone extremely fast. In fact, you throw your stone at eight kilometres per second. What happens then? Well, it will both fly forwards and fall, as before, but its curve will follow exactly the same curve as the surface of the Earth. It will fall five metres for every eight kilometres it travels. Effectively, it will fall for ever, spinning around the Earth, like the Moon. That speed, eight kilometres per second, is what's called "orbital velocity" . . .'

'How do you make something go that fast, then, sir?' asked Nikolai. 'With a cannon?'

'And that is the question!' the teacher exclaimed. 'How do you make something travel so incredibly fast? Well, yes, some people have suggested that you could use a cannon – although it would need to be a cannon almost incalculably vast. To escape the Earth's gravity altogether, you would need to fire a cannon-ball at 11.17 kilometres per second – that's thirty-two times the speed of sound! And this is not the only problem. Just suppose you do manage to build such a cannon, well, you don't want just to fire a cannonball, do you? You want to send a passenger as well. But think what would happen! To fire a cannonball big enough to contain even a single passenger, the explosion would be apocalyptic! No one could possibly survive such force! He would be crushed at once by what is known as "relative gravity" . . . In my own opinion, it may be possible to circum-vent this problem with a cannon literally hundreds of kilometres long, stretched across the surface of the Earth, and by immers-ing your passenger in some kind of protective fluid, like a baby in its mother's womb or . . .' He hesitated, struggled to find his words. 'Or, I believe that you could build a tower so tall that its head was travelling in orbit – although to be free of the Earth's gravity, such a tower would need to be 34,000 kilometres tall! An eleventh of the distance to the Moon! With traditional materials like brick and stone the lower levels would simply collapse beneath the weight of the levels above! And then, no less importantly, even if you did manage to reach space, still you would be trapped! Because in space, there is nothing! There is no air, no ground, no water! Here on Earth, we move by pushing against the ground with our feet, but in space you would be drifting helplessly – able only to revolve about your own centre of gravity!'

Konstantin paused and looked at his seven pupils, whose eyes had grown wary, their faces set with little frowns. He noticed his balloon, which was settling in the schoolyard, collapsing on its still-smouldering charcoal, and he jumped to his feet to remove the metal bowl.

'I . . . I'm sorry,' he said, returning to his bench. 'I seem to have strayed off the point.'

*

When at last two o'clock came, Konstantin gathered up his satchel and hastened back through the dusty streets – beneath plum and lime trees whose sunlit leaves were already trimmed with yellow. On Kaluzhskaya Street, he scrambled up the stairs of a house painted bright blue and white, and burst through the front door of his apartment at such a pace that a small, sand-weighted hydrogen dirigible surged away from him, spinning on the air currents. He hurried past his study, where his microscope, his barometer, his globe and his electrical dynamo made a shining line along the windowsill, stepped over the cat and arrived in Varya's bedroom, where his father-in-law was sitting on a chair beside the bed and his wife lay propped against the pillows, a ball of linen in her arms, from the end of which protruded a tiny purple face.

'My dear boy!' exclaimed the priest, embracing him fiercely, covering his face with slippery kisses. 'This is wonderful, wonderful!'

'Thank you . . .' Konstantin managed. 'Thank you, Yevgraf Nikolaievich.'

He turned to Varya, who was watching him, smiling, deep blue lines beneath her eyes. Her head lolled forwards, so that the folds beneath her chin met the sparse brown hairs on the baby's still-pointed head.

'Is . . . everything all right? Is she . . . ?'

He sat down on the bed, leant towards them.

'Here,' she said, softly.

Delicately, Konstantin collected his daughter and lay her on his forearm so that her head was enclosed by his hand. The baby stared back at him with miniature blue eyes between half-closed lids, the slight trace of eyebrows, wet lips parted round a tiny tongue, a forehead puckered as if she had just spent the morning in the bath-house. He smelt milk on her breath, the tang of fresh blood. He felt her heat, which seemed to him somehow not to be the heat of a separate body, but rather to be emanating from himself.

'Have you . . . thought about names?' called his wife, after a time.

Konstantin looked up momentarily, returned his eyes to the baby, who was trying to locate a nipple on his arm.

'I . . . I have been thinking about it,' he said.

'Would you like to name her after your mother?'

'I was thinking . . . Do you like the name Lyubov?'

'Lyubov,' she repeated, testing the syllables.

'I thought Lyubov . . . Love . . . Love is a good name for a girl, isn't it?'

September 1881

Konstantin sang to the rhythm of his oars: a cheerful tune of his own invention, which drove all thoughts out of his mind. Around him, a skittish breeze chased among the willows on the banks of the Protva, exposing the pale undersides of their yellow-green leaves. In the fields, the peasants were threshing the rye as they had threshed the rye for centuries – their flails falling in mechanical sequence. They were half a kilometre beyond the meander when Varya turned her eyes towards the high, bright clouds and Konstantin lifted the blades, felt the little wave subside around his feet. After four weeks lying in the summer air, his long, curved boat had shrunk in places, but it remained as fleet, as stable as ever, and Varya steered them easily past the tip of the peninsula, between the broad, dry beaches, the colouring alders and the walls of brambles – their silver wake dwindling as they came to a halt not a metre from the bank.

This late in the season, the algae had fallen and the eddy was motionless, clear as a spring. As Varya arranged the baby on her breast beneath her shawl, Konstantin collected the bowl that they used as a bail. He leant on the gunwale and looked past the inverted trees, the reflections of his hat and his spectacles, at the patterns of the riverbed, the thin weeds straggling towards the surface. He took a scoop of water from the boat and threw it over the prow. He threw another. And another.

'Hey!' called Varya.

Konstantin looked up to see his wife reaching for the brambles, her face translucent from her weeks of confinement. On her lap, where Lyuba sent tremors across the linen swaddling as she had lately sent tremors across the taut white skin of her mother's belly, there lay a pile of blackberries.

He returned to the gunwale to see the river plants passing at some infinitesimal velocity, contorting with minute ripples.

Again he scooped up water, but this time he hurled it as hard as he could.

'Hey!' Varya repeated.

Trembling with excitement, Konstantin threw the bail. He grabbed an oar and launched it towards the shoulder of the peninsula. He threw the second oar. He threw his seat. He shed his hat, his jacket, his spectacles and his ear trumpet into the bottom of the boat, climbed on to the prow and stood there, teetering, a foot on either gunwale while the brambles slid steadily past him.

'Kostya!'

As he dived, Konstantin felt the boat thrust away from him. He felt the freezing river meet his outstretched hands, part around his face, consume the length of his full, clothed body. He felt the bubbles boiling back towards the air, the fibrous weeds between his fingers, and when he opened his eyes he saw a team of tench flicker and vanish, a sudden squall of sunlight slice through the water, igniting the confusion on the bottom of the river as he cupped his hands and kicked out his legs like a frog.

October 1881

The flame of the candle shivered as Konstantin turned the page of his exercise book – the light repeated in the mirror on his desk, in the two, moss-caulked windows, in the coarse salt crystals dissolving slowly between them. There were no street-lamps in Borovsk. The shutters of the mole-eyed houses on Kaluzhskaya Street were closed, and beyond the glass the stars flared in the bare black sky, bright as miniature Suns. He began the next page impatiently, scrawling sentences even he could scarcely decipher, tucking notes into the margin, doodling, as he paused to think, a steam locomotive with a pair of carriages, a little Earth beneath them and a line of dots extending into space: a cosmic railway where, a moment later, he allowed the train to continue its journey at 11.17 kilometres per second – the smoke pouring aimlessly from its funnel.

Between the globe and the water bottle, Lyuba was squawk-ing discernibly, wriggling so that her small, bowed legs went one way and her shoulders went the other. Konstantin took his compass from the drawer and drew a circle on the page. Across its middle he drew a dotted ellipse to suggest the spacecraft's sphericality, while at one end of the meridional axis he drew a cylinder with a ball in its open mouth. He reached for his knife and sharpened his pencil, but then his daughter kicked a tiny foot into the chill air of the bedroom and so he leant over the basket and tucked her blankets back beneath the sheepskin.

'Lyuba . . .' he sighed. 'Now, little girl, you keep calm now. Your mother's just gone to have a rest. She will be back with your dinner very, very soon.'

Konstantin drew a second cylinder intruding from the

opposite wall of the spacecraft, which he turned into a cannon with an arsenal of cannonballs. On the polar and equatorial axes, he drew a pair of axles with a broad black disc at either end.

'Little girl . . .' he repeated.

Beneath her woollen hat, the baby's face had coloured almost violet. She was wriggling madly, her eyes sealed, her mouth open so that he could see her naked gums, her sharp little tongue. Distantly, he could hear her cry – a furious note, piercing his concentration – and, after a moment, he set down his pencil and gathered her in his arms. He held her to his chest, rolling forwards and backwards, murmuring some half-remembered lullaby until he felt her fierce, convulsive movements relax and finally stop.

When he looked again, her face had recovered its usual pink. She was watching him with round blue eyes, which seemed to express extreme surprise.

'Lyuba . . .' He lay her on his left arm, her head inside his elbow. 'Look . . . If I talk to you, will you keep calm? Please? What if I tell you a secret? How about that?' He waited, took her silence for assent. 'Very well. The secret is, you must *be* the cannon! There! What do you think of that? You see, when a cannon fires the ball goes one way and the cannon goes the other, but everybody always thinks about the ball. The fact is, when there is nothing to push against – no air, no ground, no water – then reaction is the only principle that will help you. If you want to travel in empty space, you have to eject some part of your mass. You have to fire a cannon, or a rocket, or open a barrel of compressed gas . . .'

Konstantin looked down at his daughter, who continued to watch him with wide-eyed attention – although he had barely stopped talking before he felt her beginning to stir, and so he held up his exercise book so that she would be able to see the picture.

'Very well . . .' he said, patiently. 'So, what we need is a vehicle that follows this principle. Right? The first thing to consider is that we will be travelling in a perfect void, and we will still need to breathe, so we require a craft able to withstand the pressure of an atmosphere like the atmosphere we're accustomed to here on Earth – that is, about 100 kilogrammes per square decimetre. Of course, the strongest shape is a sphere, so our craft will be spherical with a number of thick, hermetically sealed windows, allowing us to see in every direction.

'Like any other body, our craft has three mutually perpendicular axes. We will call them polar, meridional and equatorial. Now. Imagine for a moment that I am floating free in space and I remove my hat and spin it directly above me, around my polar axis. What happens? Well, I spin in the opposite direction, don't I? I spin at an angular velocity proportionate to our relative masses. And if I spin the hat around one of my transverse axes, then I will perform either a somersault or a cartwheel. So, what if our craft has a pair of wheels, which coincide precisely with the polar and equatorial axes? Well, exactly the same principle will apply! If I spin a wheel in one direction, I will revolve the craft in the opposite direction, and if I spin both wheels in the right combination I can revolve the craft to face in any direction I choose – with no loss of matter whatsoever! The only problem is, no matter how fast I spin my wheels still there will be no movement of the craft's free centre. That is to say, we will simply be revolving around the same spot. But . . .' He opened his eyes to echo the baby's expression. 'We have still got one remaining axis, haven't we? What happens if I place a reaction device at either end of the meridional axis?

'You see?' Konstantin pointed to his pair of cylinders. 'Here we have two different devices. On the right, we have a regular cannon. On the left, we have a device very like a cannon, but with a single ball attached to a very long string so that the mass is not lost. It allows us to perform journeys over a limited area. Of course, each of these devices allows us to travel in one direction only, *but* if I turn the wheels on the polar and equatorial axes then I can revolve the craft to face any direction I like! I can take a sight on a star – Aldebaran, for example – and once we are correctly orientated I can fire the cannon and we will travel at a constant velocity in exactly that direction, unless I turn the craft and fire the cannon again! And we can travel exactly as fast as we want! This is the wonder of it! We can fire again and again, and each time we will accelerate, but at a rate entirely tolerable by the human organism!'

Once again, he looked at his daughter, whose face had softened during her six weeks of independent existence, become smooth and precise. Thick, dark hair protruded from her hat. She had extracted an arm from her patchwork blanket and was reaching for his beard with tiny, pink-nailed fingers.

'But this bit is even cleverer, little wriggler!' He lifted her to his face, rubbed her nose with his own. 'You see, we want to travel in our vehicle, don't we? And what happens when our passengers move around? Well, every time they touch some part of the craft then they will move it, and if we're not very, very careful then soon we will all be tumbling head over heels! So . . . What to do? Well, what about our polar and equatorial wheels? Think for a moment. The greater the angular velocity of a wheel, the harder it becomes for the movements of a humble human to affect either its axis or its plane of rotation. Right? So, let's divide these two axles in half and attach four pistons, each one driving one of the wheels. That means that we have two pairs of wheels revolving in opposite directions but with exactly the same angular velocity! You see? Unless we alter the velocity of one or other wheel, our craft will retain the same orientation – but it will be impervious to any bumps and knocks!'

Konstantin collected his pencil and, cradling the baby in his left arm, he drew carefully a figure inside the spacecraft, attached to the wall by a long, weaving tether.

'Here we are,' he said, eagerly. 'This is me. I am looking out of the window, checking our course. And down here . . .' He drew a second figure towards the bottom of the sphere. 'This is your mother. I know it looks like she is standing on her head, but in space there is no up and down so she is perfectly comfortable, don't worry. So, having taken a sighting on Aldebaran, I am calling out the degrees and the direction that we need to revolve and she is altering the velocity of one of the wheels to correct our orientation. And over here . . .' He drew a third figure, this one in a seated position. 'This is your grandfather. It's the evening so he is having his doze – except that in weightlessness there is no need for a chair. In weightlessness, you can sit wherever you like! Space itself is an excellent chair and a splendid bed! And down here . . .' He added one more figure, standing against the hull of the spacecraft, staring towards them, arms outstretched. 'This is you. I have made you a bit bigger than you are at the moment, because we're talking about the future here, aren't we? Here you are, kicking away for all you're worth, but with our four special wheels our orientation remains completely unaffected! We will continue as straight as a comet!'

Konstantin turned his eyes towards the window where the glimmering spark of Aldebaran was following the Pleiades into the stark autumn sky. He looked down at his daughter, went to say more, but somewhere between Earth and the stars the little girl had fallen asleep.

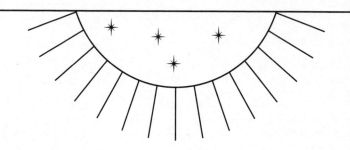

Celestial Mechanics

March 1965

Orbiting the Earth with an apogee of 495 kilometres and a perigee of 173 kilometres, Alexei Arkhipovich Leonov and Pavel Ivanovich Belyayev began their preparations for the spacewalk. Leonov closed the visor of his helmet, unstrapped himself from his couch, lifted himself with the lightest touch and hung in the air to attach his backpack oxygen system. He lay against the wall to allow Belyayev to activate the airlock, which inflated from the hull outside the hatch. Even without the Vostok ejection seat and the reserve parachute, it was difficult for the cosmonauts to move inside the capsule, which had, in the first instance, been designed for a single passenger. With the instrument panel, the radio, the television camera, the exit system primary-control panel and the two-day supply of puréed food, there was scarcely even room for the two men's couches.

Once Leonov was breathing pure oxygen, driving the nitrogen of the Earth-like atmosphere from his bloodstream, he unfastened the umbilical connecting his pressure suit to the spacecraft's life-support system and waited for Belyayev to equalize the pressure in the airlock. As ever, the commander's movements were calm, unhurried. His dark eyes were narrow beneath his heavy black eyebrows and the red insignia on his white domed helmet.

'Ready!' said Leonov, and gave himself a spin around his polar axis so that the couches and the instruments went parading around him.

Belyayev's lips moved between the mandibles of his microphones.

'Patience, my friend,' said his deep, Vologda voice in Leonov's headset.

At last, the commander gave the signal and Leonov turned transversely to face the hatch in the wall beside his couch, which he opened to reveal a rubber tube 2.5 metres long. The Volga airlock comprised forty inflatable aerobooms in three separate sections, any one of which could have failed without compromising the integrity of the structure. Along the lower side, there was a pair of handrails, which Leonov followed as he floated towards the outer hatch, the lights and the waiting cine-camera. He checked that the light filter on his helmet was in the correct position, consulted the pressure gauge beneath the buttoned flap on his right sleeve and attached the safety tether. He bent forwards in the narrow space to see Belyayev salute, and when the hatch was sealed he watched the gauge in the wall beside him as the pressure in the airlock equalized with the pressure in his spacesuit – 0.4 atmosphere – and finally reduced to a vacuum.

When the exterior hatch folded towards him, Leonov might have been facing the flame of an arc-welder. He lowered his eyes instinctively, collected the cine-cinema, grasped the handle.

'I'm pushing off!' he said.

'Not so fast, you . . .' said Belyayev. He repeated a series of numbers: Leonov's pulse and rate of respiration, which were relayed through the EKG sensors and the ohmic transmitter strapped around his chest. 'Very well, Lyosh. The vital signs are fine. You have the order to go. Good luck!'

At 0834 UTC on 18 March 1965, the first spacewalker emerged into open space. Blinking in the silver-white sunlight, he attached the cine-camera to the frame of the hatch, then pushed again and felt the spacecraft move away from him – lightly, like pushing a child on a swing. At first, floating backwards, he saw only the yellow shaft of the airlock, which protruded from the spherical capsule and the equipment module, a retro-engine at either end of their meridional axis. To his surprise, there was no sharp contrast between their light and shadow – all parts seemed to be illuminated equally, as if the ship were bathing in the Sun itself – and as he reached the end of his 5.35-metre tether and turned around his polar axis he saw the reason.

Leonov saw the Earth.

Far to his left, where the planet curved into the haze of the atmosphere, he saw the brilliant, cloud-patterned green of Europe. He saw the Straits of Gibraltar and the tawny expanse of the Sahara Desert. He saw the Black Sea, blue within its sunlit coastline, the tiny inlet of Novorossiysk Harbour and the little rift of the Dardanelles. Through fissures in the light-grey clouds, he saw the snow-shining heads of the Ural Mountains, their valleys, their ravines, even their streams. Turning slowly, he saw the Universe, the violet sky becoming velvet black, the fearless stars in the illimitable void.

Leonov opened his arms like wings.

'Blondie!' From the cosmic silence, there came the bright, distinctive voice of Yuri Alexeyevich Gagarin. 'How are you feeling?'

The cosmonaut gazed at the Kuban Steppe.

'Yuri . . .' he managed. 'I can see so much!'

'Do you feel equal to this challenge?'

'I . . . I can see so far!'

Leonov watched the Earth sail past him at 28,000 km/h – 7.8 km/s – the fringes of Europe fall into the belts of red, blue and orange that ringed the horizon, the Siberian forest extend as far as he could see, riven by its rivers: the Ob, the Yenisei, the Lena. He tried to locate Kemerovo, the city where he had lived as a boy, but he was unable to identify any trace of humanity at all.

It was only when he reached for the switch on his thigh, to activate his chest-mounted camera, that Leonov realized he had a problem. In the absolute vacuum the spacesuit had ballooned, and it was all he could do to return his arms to his sides. With a tremendous effort, he bent his legs to reduce the suit's internal volume, but still he was completely unable to lean forwards, and suddenly the spacecraft was approaching at such an alarming velocity that he could only just keep his helmet clear and soften the blow with his hands. At once, he found himself moving in the opposite direction, spinning about his transversal axis, his arms pinned open in their helpless impression of flight.

They were at the most northerly point of their orbit, leaving the forest for the glistening wealth of the Pacific Ocean, when Belyayev issued the instruction to return to the airlock. Bending his legs, Leonov managed to grasp the tether between his gloves and pull himself in the direction of the spacecraft. As if working a weight machine, he released the camera from its mounting and pushed it into the hatch, but he had barely turned to follow it feet first, according to the programme, when he found it floating back out again and he was forced to revolve to retrieve it. By now, the cosmonaut was growing tired. Despite the reflective oversuit, a relief valve to vent excess heat and moisture and a layer of constantly moving liquid coolant, he could feel the sweat the length of his body. In desperation, he caught the camera once more and returned it to the airlock, but however hard he tried to angle himself correctly he found it impossible to do the same.

Another minute passed before Leonov decided to reduce the pressure in his spacesuit. Groaning with the strain, he managed to bring his left arm the whole way across his body and reach the valve beneath the flap on his right sleeve. He haemorrhaged oxygen until the gauge read 0.3 atmosphere, but still he was unable to bring his legs together and again he released the valve, to the safety limit of 0.27.

'Lyosha?' called Belyayev. The orientation system was struggling to absorb his movements. 'Lyosha, talk to me! What's happening?'

The sweat was floating into Leonov's helmet, clouding his visor until the ring of the hatch was almost invisible. His breath was a gale in his ears. He fought so violently that his gloves were forced away from his hands and his boots were forced off his feet. In theory, he knew, it was possible for the commander to decompress the spacecraft and enter the airlock himself to help him, but already his oxygen system had reached a critical level and, besides, the electronics were designed to operate in normal atmospheric pressures and temperatures, not in a vacuum, and he had serious doubts that they had sufficient nitrogen and oxygen on board even to recompress the cabin. He had no time for hesitation or consultation. With the hard, lifeless fingers of his left glove, he reached again for the valve on his arm and, with decompression sickness now almost a certainty, he reduced the pressure still further, past the safety limit, to 0.25 atmosphere.

Through the mist that drifted before his eyes, Leonov saw his wife, Svetlana, and their four-year-old daughter, Vika, together in their garden in Moscow. He saw the blue sky above him and the neatly mown grass beneath his feet. He squeezed his arms together and began to pull himself into the airlock head first, scrabbling at the hatch, the handles, the smooth rubber sides. At last, he felt his helmet clack against the metal hull of the capsule, but still he faced the near-impossible task of revolving his 1.9-metre length in the tube's 1.2-metre diameter to close the exterior hatch. The cosmonaut was on the edge of heatstroke. He could see nothing, feel only dimly. His ears were full of the sloshing of his sweat, the machine-gun thunder of his heart. Doubling forwards, he jammed himself into the little space. He kicked against his useless boots, dragged himself centimetre by centimetre back the way he had come.

'Thank God,' breathed the commander, as Leonov floated back into the cabin.

*

It was another twenty-two hours, and sixteen orbits, before a tracking station in the Far East sent instructions to *Voskhod 2* to re-enter the atmosphere. Strapped to their couches, Leonov and Belyayev waited for the jolt of the retro-rockets, which would slow the ship's tumbling progress. In moments, through the porthole in the hatch, Leonov saw the Pacific Ocean give way to the magnificent vertebrae of the Andes, the lustrous green of the Brazilian rainforest, the horizon fiery with yet another sunset. He saw once more the delicate coastline and the gaping Atlantic, the giant coils of the currents and the sudden sparks of islands. For fifteen hours, neither of the two cosmonauts had stirred from his couch. On Leonov's return to the cabin, the second hatch had failed to seal correctly and the environmental control system had compensated by flooding the atmosphere with oxygen. Even with the temperature reduced from 18°C to 15°C to reduce humidity, the slightest spark from the electronics or the glancing blow of a boot ring could have caused a conflagration.

As *Voskhod 2* entered its sixteenth night, it was cold and dark and lonely.

'Diamond!' Gagarin used the call-sign. 'Congratulations, boys! Where did you land?'

There was a moment before Belyayev replied.

'The landing system has malfunctioned, Yuri Alexeyevich.' His voice contained the slightest tremor. 'We believe that the solar orientation sensor was damaged by the pyrotechnic gases when we jettisoned the airlock. We have lost stability. The pressure in the air tanks has fallen beneath twenty-five atmospheres. Oxygen levels are critical and we only have enough fuel to make one attempt at re-entry. We request emergency mode.'

As they waited for a response, the cosmonauts shared a desultory dinner: four 160-gramme tubes of meat purée and two 160-gramme tubes of chocolate sauce. They watched the darkly glowing Earth give way rhythmically to the multitude of lifeless stars.

'Emergency mode has been authorized, Diamond,' said another voice finally, as the Sun rose again above the rim of the planet. 'You are instructed to perform a manual re-entry on either the eighteenth or the twenty-second orbit.'

In its original design, the single couch in the Vostok capsule had faced the Vzor optical orientation device in the porthole, but such were the difficulties of including an additional passenger that the technicians had turned the cabin's interior through ninety degrees. It was apparent at once that even Leonov would be unable to reach the controls from his seat. Tentatively, the two men unstrapped themselves. They arranged themselves in a variety of positions before Leonov found himself squeezed into the narrow space underneath the couches, holding Belyayev by the waist so that he was able to focus on the periscope.

The Vzor was an ingenious invention: a central view surrounded by a ring of eight round ports, which would light up simultaneously when the craft was correctly aligned to the Sun. Trapped on his back, Leonov could see the instrument reflected faintly in the visor of the commander's helmet – his dark eyes shrunk now almost into slits. He held him steady, breathed as evenly as possible. Belyayev was a pilot of ability and experience. In the twenty years since the war in the Pacific, he had flown every model of Soviet jet plane – although even a MiG-21 could barely achieve a twentieth of the velocity of *Voskhod 2* and, besides, an aircraft was governed by the laws of aerodynamics, with a single, two-axis hand-control column, whereas a spacecraft was governed by celestial mechanics, requiring two three-axis controllers. The stakes could hardly have been greater. Too steep a re-entry angle and they would burn up in seconds, like a meteorite. Too shallow an angle and they would simply glance off the upper atmosphere, like a stone off the surface of a pond, and remain in space to suffocate or starve.

It took forty-six seconds for the cosmonauts to return to their couches and restore the craft's centre of gravity, and for Belyayev to fire the braking engine. They felt the shock of the retro-rocket. They counted down the seconds until the instrument module separated from their re-entry module, felt its shudder, but still it was as if some force was holding them, slowing them down, and as Leonov turned to the porthole he saw, to his horror, that a bundle of wires continued to connect the two modules. As they fell into the thermosphere, they were spinning around one another with a growing velocity, like a centrifuge. For a time, he was conscious of the sunlight blinking, filling the cabin in instants. He saw the gauge reach 10 g-forces, the thermometer register external temperatures of 1000°C, but then his vision began to narrow, to grey, and he was able to see nothing but the molten metal that poured across the glass like luminous raindrops.

*

Around them rose a forest of conifers and birch trees. The capsule was trapped between a pair of enormous firs, black, steaming, settling steadily in the neck-deep snow until the landing hatch resembled the door of a cave. Above them, the parachute hung in the wind-torn treetops, red and flapping. Among the four-toed tracks of hare and fox in a nearby clearing, the antennae intended to relay their location lay broken, glinting in the thin afternoon sunlight.

Through eyes red with broken blood vessels, Leonov consulted the orientation gauges in the cabin, which had rolled through 180 degrees on landing so that he was forced to kneel between the switches and the instrument panel on the ceiling. They had, it seemed, missed their landing site by some 2,000 kilometres. They were approximately 180 kilometres north-east of the city of Perm, lost in the Siberian wilderness.

A Siberian himself, Leonov knew well the dangers of the forest in late winter. Following Belyayev into the freezing air, he removed his helmet and his rigid oversuit and began systematically to strip himself naked. He emptied the knee-deep sweat from his boots. He wrung out the thermal protection layers, the inner comfort layers and the Dederon undersuit. He unstrapped the waterproof circuitry that encircled the dense blond hair on his chest, discarded the probes and redressed as quickly as he could.

It was early that evening when the cosmonauts heard the clatter of an approaching helicopter. Abandoning their fire, they struggled across the snow to a clearing and stood, waving wildly, as a civilian aircraft emerged from the treetops – its downdraught indistinguishable from the gale. A face appeared at the door in the side, shouting inaudibly. A rope ladder fell towards them, thin and flailing, but even without the oversuits it was plain to both men that it would never support their weight. They watched the pilot try to squeeze his rotor blades between the trees. They watched a bottle of cognac come arching through the air and smash against a tree trunk. They watched two wolfskin coats and two pairs of heavy trousers become entangled in the branches.

In the failing light, Leonov and Belyayev fought with the lines of the parachute, tried to drag it to the ground to use as a blanket. Beyond its deep red folds, the sky had flooded with grey-black clouds and when it started to snow they retreated once more to the fire, which they had built against a birch tree, where the snow was shallow and there was some little shelter from the surrounding drifts. They sat, small and shivering, as the forest vanished tree by tree into the darkness, listening to the rifle crack of the ice in the branches, the animal roar of the gale, the hiss of the flames, which whipped and turned, scarcely warmer than themselves.

'Wolves!' said Belyayev, softly. It was the first time that either of them had spoken since sunset.

Leonov glanced at the sphere of the capsule, the retro-engine jutting dark above the gaping hole of the hatch. He looked into the forest and, faint through the falling snow, saw a pair of fire-coloured lights. Whatever the emergency, both men had agreed not to use their torches, in case of the need to signal to an aircraft, and so he reached into the fire for the longest branch, which he held in the air to see a contracting circle of low, grey figures: a pack emaciated by the winter, their jaws apart, their webbed feet moving effortlessly across the snow.

'They won't . . .' he started.

'They will,' Belyayev corrected him.

'Yes,' said Leonov. 'They will.'

'Keep them back,' said the commander.

The leader was a great, gaunt male, his pale hair bristling, his shoulders as broad as Leonov's own. As the cosmonauts backed away from the fire, he followed them at a distance of barely three metres. When Leonov waved the branch, the wolf flinched his long face sideways, but still he continued to come, while his companions closed from every direction, their sharp teeth slavering, bright with the sputtering flame.

'Now!' Belyayev shouted.

Leonov threw himself towards the capsule. He slipped, wallowed in the snow, but the opening was low and he dived on to the invisible instruments as the commander dragged the hatch back on to the scorched stumps of the explosive bolts.

In the light of their final match, the instruments still reported that they were 180 kilometres north-east of Perm, deep in the Siberian wilderness. The thermometer informed them that it was minus 30°C. In their flimsy spacesuits, the cosmonauts huddled together on the hard, freezing ceiling. They breathed until the atmosphere in the cabin was heavy and poisonous, and then, the length of the long night, they took turns to hold the hatch ajar – open enough to allow in the air, closed enough to keep out the dribbling, unseen muzzles of the wolves, who screamed like the wind and tore with their teeth and their claws at the tortured metal.

Author's Note

Although this book is a novel, it is based on actual people and events.

In 1903, Konstantin Tsiolkovsky published his paper 'The Investigation of World Spaces by Reactive Vehicles' in the St Petersburg journal *Science Review*. Developing the principles that he had first explored in his unpublished 1883 manuscript 'Free Space', and including the basic equation for rocket flight (the 'Tsiolkovsky Equation'), it is universally acknowledged to be the first theoretically sound proof of the viability of space travel. It was not, however, until after the Russian Revolution that Tsiolkovsky's work became widely known even inside Russia – by which time the American Robert Goddard and the German-Hungarian Hermann Oberth were working independently towards similar conclusions. In 1918, Tsiolkovsky was elected a member of the Socialist Academy and, in 1921, he was awarded a lifetime pension, allowing him to devote himself fully to his scientific passions. Among his seminal ideas were the use of liquid hydrogen/liquid oxygen fuel in rockets, multistage rockets, space stations, space elevators, airlocks, pressurized space suits, gyroscopes to control orientation and closed cycle biological systems to support space colonies. He lived to inspire, meet and correspond with Valentin Glushko, Mikhail Tikhonravov, Sergei Korolev and other key architects of the Soviet space programme. He died in 1935, the author of more than five hundred works of science, science fiction and mystical philosophy, and received a state funeral in his adopted town of Kaluga.

His wife, Varvara, the mother of his seven children, survived him by five years.

His daughter and assistant, Lyubov, lived until 1957 – in which year the launch of *Sputnik 1* was timed to mark the centenary of Tsiolkovsky's birth.

Nikolai Fedorov remained a librarian until his death in 1903 – first in the Rumyantsev Museum Library, then in the Moscow Archives of the Ministry of Foreign Affairs. A prolific, but private and chaotic writer, his works of 'cosmic' philosophy were edited posthumously and published as *The Philosophy of the Common Task* (1908 and 1913).

Alexei Leonov returned to space in 1975 as Soviet commander for the Apollo-Soyuz Test Project, the first joint US/Soviet space flight. He remained in orbit for nearly six days, and landed without incident near Baikonur Cosmodrome in Kazakhstan. He later served as deputy director of the Yuri Gagarin Cosmonaut Training Centre. General Leonov retired in 1991, and now lives in Moscow.

Acknowledgements

I must thank Charlotte and Edwyn for years of support and enthusiasm, for listening so patiently and advising so thoughtfully as I read *Konstantin* aloud yet again. Jenny and Willy have been consistently brilliant. Olla, Rose and Cai have been invaluable – especially in Russian matters, and in spite of Olla's passion for Rick Wakeman's *The Six Wives of Henry VIII*.

This book would never have been written without the guidance of Clare Alexander.

Boundless thanks must also go to Mary Mount, Sarah Coward, Literature Wales, Natania Jansz, Mark Ellingham, Brian Chikwava, James Miller, Matthew Scudamore, Paul Binding, Helena Attlee, Jasper Fforde, Chris Stewart, the British Interplanetary Society, the forbearing staff of Brecon Library, and Niall Griffiths, who had thoughts about sympathy at just the right time.

He just wanted a decent book to read ...

Not too much to ask, is it? It was in 1935 when Allen Lane, Managing Director of Bodley Head Publishers, stood on a platform at Exeter railway station looking for something good to read on his journey back to London. His choice was limited to popular magazines and poor-quality paperbacks – the same choice faced every day by the vast majority of readers, few of whom could afford hardbacks. Lane's disappointment and subsequent anger at the range of books generally available led him to found a company – and change the world.

'We believed in the existence in this country of a vast reading public for intelligent books at a low price, and staked everything on it'
Sir Allen Lane, 1902–1970, founder of Penguin Books

The quality paperback had arrived – and not just in bookshops. Lane was adamant that his Penguins should appear in chain stores and tobacconists, and should cost no more than a packet of cigarettes.

Reading habits (and cigarette prices) have changed since 1935, but Penguin still believes in publishing the best books for everybody to enjoy. We still believe that good design costs no more than bad design, and we still believe that quality books published passionately and responsibly make the world a better place.

So wherever you see the little bird – whether it's on a piece of prize-winning literary fiction or a celebrity autobiography, political tour de force or historical masterpiece, a serial-killer thriller, reference book, world classic or a piece of pure escapism – you can bet that it represents the very best that the genre has to offer.

Whatever you like to read – trust Penguin.